THE DESERTER

by Nigel Gray

Illustrated by Ted Lewin

Harper & Row, Publishers
New York, Hagerstown, San Francisco, London

FIRST EDITION

Library of Congress Cataloging in Publication Data
Gray, Nigel.
    The deserter.

    SUMMARY: Four English children form a close
friendship with a young deserter from the British
army and help him escape from the authorities.
[1. Friendship—Fiction.   2. England—Fiction]
I. Lewin, Ted.   II. Title.
PZ7.G7813De   [Fic]   76–58693
ISBN 0–06–022061–9
ISBN 0–06–022062–7 lib. bdg.

TH

THE DESERTER

J
G
Gray, Nigel
The deserter

J
G
Gray, Nigel
The deserter

For Sara and Jo,
Kathryne, Andrew, Lucy and Alice

ONE

It was the summer holidays when it happened. The summer holidays are always the best time of the year. I like them better than Christmas or anything. But that summer was more special than any other time in my life. Something happened that I'll never forget. Only I won't tell you about all that yet. I'll tell you about when we first went to the island.

It was a really nice summer that year. Ever so sunny. But it was near the end of the holidays and we were bored. My friend Terry and me played out on the street nearly all the time. Sometimes we went up to the park or along the canal.

Once when we were up by the canal we got a ride on this boat. You know them boats people hire for their holidays that go up and down the canal. Well, me and Terry were up by the canal and this boat came by. And Terry shouts out, "Give us a ride, Mister." And this fellow says, "All right."

There were four guys on the boat, and they pulled over to the side, under the bridge where it's deepest, and me and Terry got on. It was great. They don't go very fast though. But they let us have a go steering. There's not much steering to do really because canals just go straight most of the time. It was nice anyway. We just went along. Up past the old mill that's empty. Past where the swans always are. Past the big mill and the hospital, and right on out to where the town ends. They put us off then because they said it was a long walk back.

They were real nice. One of the guys said that he used to play by the canal when he was a kid. Not our canal. A canal near where he used to live. He said there was still barges then. And sometimes him and his mates used to get a ride on one of the barges. Another one said that they still had barges in Germany. Not on little canals, but on big rivers. He said he'd worked on one that went from Holland right up to Switzerland. Anyway they put us off and we walked back. It was a long way. But it wasn't too long. It was good.

But most days nothing special like that happened. Most of the time it was just boring. But it was better than going to school. Just about anything's better than going to school.

Then there was this Sunday and my dad didn't have to go to work. It was a really sunny day and my dad said we were going to go to Treasure Island. Not a real Treasure Island. He just called it Treasure Island.

I went and got Terry. He nearly always came with us if I went out with my mum and dad. His mum and dad never took him out anywhere. Then my sister started moaning. She's not my real sister. But she's like my sister. It's like my mum's not my real mum. My real mum went away. I asked my dad why, but he wouldn't ever tell me nothing. This mum I've got now and my dad just live together. I've got my dad and Christine's got her mum. But we all sort of live together like one family.

Christine's all right. She's older than me but I'm nearly as strong as her. We fight sometimes, but not too much. We get on all right really. Anyway, this time Christine started moaning and said it wasn't fair if Terry was coming because she'd be on her own. So Mum said why didn't she ask one of her friends. She said she'd had a quarrel with them so Mum said she'd better go and make it up then. So she went and got Lucy from down the road.

Lucy's all right. She's more of a sort of tomboy than Christine. She'll do anything. The way to get her mad is to call her Juicy Lucy. She hates that. There's this fat kid at school called James who's a real bully, and once he was calling her Juicy Lucy and she slogged him one and made his nose bleed. I don't call her that much though. It only upsets her. Anyway I don't want to get a nosebleed.

4

It's funny how people get upset by names. My sister's name used to be Nicola but everybody called her Knickers and she used to come home from school crying. So she changed her name to Christine. My name's Andrew. Everybody calls me Andy. Sometimes they call me Bandy Andy, or Andy Pandy, but I don't care.

Anyway we all piled into my dad's old station wagon. We slung in the swimming things and towels and spades and everything. Then Dad put this box in the back. We all kept wanting to know what was in the box but my mum just kept saying, "Never you mind what's in there. Just you leave it alone. It's nothing to do with you." Then Christine said, "Where's Dad gone?" and Mum said, "You're too full of questions, you are. Just wait a minute."

Then I saw him coming out of old Jimmy's house up the street. Old Jimmy had a garden up by the railway and my dad came out with one of Jimmy's spades. He put it in the back and then got into the driver's seat.

"What's that for, Dad?"

"Never you mind," he said. "You'll see."

"Can we stop and get some sweets?" I said.

"No, we can't."

"Why not?" Christine said. "It's not fair. I've got my own money."

"Never mind about that," my dad said. "You hang on to it. It'll come in handy later in the week."

My dad's like that. Sometimes he's great. Another time he won't even listen.

We drove out of town down the river. Then we turned off the road and went down this lane, and we came out in some woods. My dad parked the car and we all piled out.

"Go on, you lot," my dad said. "Take your things and go down them steps and you'll come to the river."

"Go and have a swim," said Mum.

"That's right. On with you, now," he said.

"Aren't you coming, Dad?"

"No. Me and Mum have got something else to do."

"Oh go on. It's much more fun when you come."

"We'll have a swim with you later. Go on. Clear off now."

We knew something was up because he wasn't saying it cross or anything. You can tell when my dad's cross halfway up the street. And Mum was smiling. She was in on what was going on, all right. So we went down these giant steps to the water. We got into our swimming suits and went in. It was freezing. We played for a bit and then we heard the car horn honking and my dad calling. We ran up the giant stairs. Great steps carved out of the rock. We were puffing and blowing when we got to the top.

My dad said, "If you want to find the treasure, first you've got to find the island, and then look for a clue."

"What treasure?" said Christine.

"Oh, just a small treasure."

"But where's the island?" I said.

"Well, where do you think an island would be?" Dad said.

"There's a traffic island in the High Street," said Terry. He's always saying things like that in school and making me laugh and then we both get into trouble.

"Off you go then," said Dad. "You go and look there." I stared at him. I didn't know what to think.

"Well," he said. "Where else do you have islands, besides the High Street?"

"In the river," said Lucy.

"Yeah, yeah, in the river," we all shouted, and we turned and began to run down the steps again.

"Hang about!" Dad shouted after us. We all stopped running and turned around to look back up at him. "You've just been down there," he said. "Did you see any islands down there?"

We looked at each other. Then at him. "No."

"Then use your noddles."

"Oh come on Dad. Where is it?"

"Use your noddles," he said again and grinned at us. We looked around. There was the track that the car had come down. But that just led back to the road. Then the

8

steps down to the river where we'd been. But there was no island down there. Christine climbed up on a wall.

"I can see right up the river," she said, "and there's no island up that way."

"It must be down here then," Lucy said. She was right. There was only one other way. There was a narrow footpath leading into the woods.

"Is it down there, Dad?" I asked. But he just smiled and shrugged.

"Yeah. It's down here. It's down here. Come on."

We ran down the path. Lucy was in front till I caught up with her and gave her a shove into the side. Then she caught up with me and shoved me so hard I fell into these ferns. By the time I got out the others had all gone by, and I was last. Except for Dad.

"Lucy pushed me into the bushes, Dad."

"Serves you right," he said.

I ran on as fast as I could till I nearly caught up with the others. The path wound about through the wood and then went downhill toward the river. We crossed a footbridge that had a lot of planks missing. I could see down to the stream bed underneath. It was all dry then. There hadn't been any rain for ages. The path got steeper and the trees further apart and then Lucy yelled, "There it is! There it is!"

"Where?"

"There. Look!"

"Oh yeah."

"There's the island. There's the island."

"And there's Mum."

The river curved around this bend, like an elbow. And tucked right in the crook of the elbow was the island. It was right close to our bank. And there was a fallen tree that made a bridge from the bank to the island. We all shuffled across the tree-bridge, balancing. It was scary, because if you started wobbling you couldn't stop. And if someone else was wobbling, they made you wobble. It was really good.

We all got across onto the island. It was about as long as four rooms in a row. And it was about as wide as one room. There was three trees growing out from

10

the island, hanging over the river. And there was a big old tree that had fallen down that you could walk along. All the rest was like a jungle, covered with some plant as high as me. If you crouched down no one could see you at all. The stems of the plant were round and hollow like bamboo, so it was easy to break it down with a stick to make a pathway. There was a couple of sandy places on the island where the plant wasn't growing, and there was a little beach on one end, and another on the side nearest the bank. On the other side, where the trees were, the water got deep straightaway.

We explored around for a bit, then Lucy said, "Where's the clue?"

Christine said, "It's not fair. It could be anywhere. We'll never find it."

"You'll never find it if you don't look for it," Mum said.

Christine said, "I know. You've buried it. That's why you brought that spade."

"No," Dad said. "The clue's not buried."

So we all started looking around. I

started looking up this tree. I climbed up the tree and the branches hung out over the water. It was like being on a boat. I could look down and see the water underneath me. You could see all like green plants growing under the water, all waving about like a dead man's hands. And there was all this soft green moss growing on the tree branch so it was lovely and soft to sit on. I was looking down into the water and I saw some fishes. Quite small, but not ever so small. Not like minnows in the canal. These would go along slowly and then they'd suddenly dive into the plants and disappear. I was sitting on the branch in the sun watching the fishes and I forgot about the clue, and then all of a sudden Lucy shouted out, "I've found it. I've found the clue."

Christine said, "What's it say? What's it say?"

We all ran over to Lucy to see the clue, but I was last because I had a job to get down the tree.

Christine said, "Here, let me read it." She

took the clue away from Lucy. She gets
bossy like that sometimes. She took the clue
and read it out. It said:

THE TREASURE IS NEAR AT HAND
IT'S SURPRISING WHAT YOU CAN FIND IN
THE SAND

We all looked at the clue and then at
Mum and Dad.

Christine said, "What sand, Dad?" but
Mum and Dad just laughed. Then we all
tried to run to some sand and all bumped
into each other.

"Get the spades," I said.

Christine said, "Dad, can I have the big
spade?"

"That's not fair," I said.

"I asked first," said Christine.

"No one can have it," said Dad. "I've put
it back in the car."

So we had to use our own spades. Well,
when we found the box buried in the sand
we thought we'd got the treasure. But there
was a padlock on the box and in the padlock

keyhole was a rolled-up piece of paper. It was another clue.

IF YOU WANT TO UNLOCK ME
YOU MUST FIND THE KEY HOLE IN THE
DEAD TREE

Lucy and Terry ran to the trees that were growing out over the water. Lucy began looking around the bottom of one with sharp jerky movements like a mouse, while Terry was shinning up another like a monkey.

"They're not dead, stupid," said Christine.

"Well which ones are dead then?" said Terry. "Miss Clever Clogs."

I saw Christine look at the long trunk which lay across the island like an overpass. We ran to it, and the others followed. We searched along the trunk, feeling into the holes. Then Christine said, "Here it is. I've found the key." We all yelled and ran back to the box.

"Get away," said Christine. "I can't undo it if you're all crowding me."

14

"Oh come on," I said. "Open it."

She got it unlocked and opened the lid. Inside the box was a picnic. There was sandwiches and sausages and cake and apples and everything. There was four bags of sweets with our names on. And there was a little packet and it said FOR EVERYONE on it. Lucy found it so she opened it and inside was lots of like lipsticks, only all in different colors.

"Ergh! Lipstick!" said Terry.

"What's these?" I asked.

"They're face paints," Mum said.

"To make you look like Red Indians," said Dad.

"Ergh! I'm not having any of that muck on my face," said Terry. "I'd look like a woman."

"Well you needn't," said Dad. "I'm going to. Chuck them over here, Chris."

Dad started to draw some lines on his face with the red stick. "Here, Joan," he said to Mum, "do me face for me, will you?" So Mum drew these fantastic patterns on Dad's face. He looked great.

"Do me next, Mum," I said. So she did

me. And then Christine. Dad did Lucy. And then Terry wanted war paint on as well. And then Dad did Mum. And then we all looked like Red Indians.

So we had our picnic. We made a fire with some sticks. We put stones around so the fire wouldn't spread. Then we piled up the sticks in the middle and put our sandwich papers underneath. We got a fire going and fried the sausages. It was great.

After that we played. In the water. All around the island. We played till we got really hungry again. We hadn't brought anything for supper so we had to pack up then and go home. We tried to wash the mud off our legs in the river but the water was really cold. Then we walked back up the path to the car. We packed all the stuff away and got in. But then the car wouldn't start. Our car's always going wrong. My dad always reckons he can mend cars, but when he's finished mending them they're usually worse than when he started. So we all got out again and Dad fiddled about under the hood.

Mum said, "I don't know why you don't

get rid of that old car." Dad didn't say anything. Mum said, "You spend more time messing about with that . . ."

"Look, I've told you before." Dad poked his head out from under the hood. "If I sell this I'll get about a hundred and twenty pounds for it. What could I buy for that? I'd just get another heap of old junk that was always going wrong, wouldn't I."

"Well at least you've admitted it's a heap of old junk at last," Mum said.

Mum didn't say anything else. She just wandered off and started picking flowers and leaves and that. The rest of us started playing hide-and-seek. But when Christine was supposed to be hiding her eyes she must have been looking because I'd got a great place and she found me straightaway. She said she wasn't, but she must have been. So I stopped playing and went to watch Dad.

"What's the matter with the car, Dad?" I said.

He didn't say anything for a bit. Once he gets his head in an engine you might as well talk to the steering wheel. Then he said,

"It's nothing. It's just a fuse." He had a tiny glass tube in his hand. He showed me. There was a little wire up the middle which was broken, and the glass was burned. "We'll have to walk into town," he said.

So me and Dad went into town. It wasn't all that far. But I was starving.

"Can we get something to eat, Dad?"

"No," he said. "We'll have to wait till we get home."

"Why?"

"Because we can't afford to eat out, that's why," he said. "It won't take us long. If we can find a garage open."

When we got into town people kept giving us funny looks. Some people were laughing at us. I saw them. I didn't know why. I took hold of Dad's hand. He looked down at me to see what was the matter. Then he started to laugh. Then I noticed he'd still got all his war paint on. And so had I. That's why the people were looking at us.

"I'm glad I've got you with me," said Dad. "Otherwise I'd feel a right Charlie."

We found a garage that was open and Dad

bought a fuse. Then we went back and he put it in the car and we drove home. It was a great day. We all thought it would be the best day of the whole summer. But we didn't know what was going to happen next.

TWO

It was one day in the last week of the holidays. Terry and me and Christine and Lucy went up to play by the canal. Terry had a net and a jam jar and tried to catch some minnows. He let me have a go. But when I tried to shove the net in front of the fish, the water held it back. I suppose the water is a friend to the fish really. Terry hid his net in the long grass and we chucked the jam jar into the canal and threw stones at it. Then we wandered along the bank. Some cabin cruisers came along and Terry called out, "Give us a lift," but no one did. We passed the bridge where a kid from our street fell in and drowned. Whenever I pass that bridge it makes me feel sort of watery inside my stomach. A bit further up there's a foot-bridge over the canal. Spotty Sally was up on the bridge. She's a black dog from our street. She had her head through the railings and she was crying because there's no way straight down and she wanted to come with us. It was sad. It was gray and cloudy and not very warm. We didn't know what to do. We just walked on up the bank, chucking things in the canal. Then Lucy said, "Hey, look at the mill."

On the other bank there was a huge crane by the old mill. The mill's roof had been taken off and there was a man standing on top of the wall holding on to the crane with one hand and pushing the stones off the wall with his other hand and his foot. The stones were falling and then crashing onto the ground and each time a cloud of dust billowed up. We ran along the towpath till we came as close as we could get. Then we stood watching. The man was moving slowly along the top of the wall pushing the stones off. He came to a great big stone across the top of a window. He loosened and pushed away the stones at each side till the big stone on top was left balanced on the window frame. Then he pushed at it but it was too heavy. He couldn't move it. He kept changing his position and trying again. Then he climbed down the crane and the man in the cab handed him out an iron bar. He climbed right up again and stood on top of the wall. He started to work with his crowbar at the stones at the side of the window frame and some of them started to fall. And then the frame started to collapse ever so slowly. The man straightened up quickly and held on to the crane with both hands, and the big stone across the top slowly tipped out into space like on the television when they show things in slow motion. And then it fell. The wall was ever so high. Much higher than a house. And the big stone just fell through the air and then crunched onto the ground and a great column of dust rose slowly up into the air.

It was great to watch. It must have felt funny standing up there in the sky and knocking the wall where you were standing out from under your feet. But even that was sort of sad in a way too. I mean that mill had always been there since I came to live in this town and I liked it being there, really. Then Christine said, "Let's go in the houses."

On our side of the canal, opposite the old mill, they'd been pulling down all the houses. Hundreds of them. It was a big open space with almost nothing on it except parked cars and trucks, with rubbish and broken glass all over the place. But here and there some of the old houses were still standing. I don't know why. My dad says the people from the town council don't know their ass from their elbow half the time. The council workmen had bricked up all the downstairs doors and windows to try to stop kids getting in. But we could still get in if we wanted. Right by the canal, just over the wall, were four of these houses in a row. We often played in them.

We shinned over the wall. These particular houses we got into by going down the coal hole on the front wall into the cellar and then up the stairs. Christine and Lucy got down first. Then Terry. I slid down the coal chute into the dark cellar. I never did like going through them cellars in the dark. It gave me the creeps. You had to feel with your hand across the wall, and the wall was always slimy and wet. So I let Terry go in front and I just held on to him and let him feel along the wall to the stairs. The ground floor was dim because it had been bricked up, so we'd go upstairs into what used to be the bedrooms.

Lucy said, "Let's watch the men on the mill from the window."

Terry and me ran up the stairs after the girls. The stairs were just bare wood. The wallpaper was hanging off and the plaster had crumbled and it crunched under our feet. We went into the back bedroom. Christine and Lucy were pulling down some old cloth that had been hung over the window.

I said, "Who stuck that up there?"

Lucy said, "How should I know?"

They pulled it down and the room got light and we could see out across the canal. The man was still on top of the wall and the crane engine was still droning on. We saw another big stone fall and hit the ground. *Crump!*

Then I heard a noise behind us. The others heard it too.

It was like a slithering sort of noise. I turned around and there was a man lying on the floor. Like a tramp. Only he was young. And the slithering noise was, he'd dragged himself along the floor into the doorway so we couldn't get out of the room. One of us yelled. I don't know which one. It might even have been me. I felt all the hairs prickling on the back of my neck and I felt as though I'd got goose pimples all over my body. I was really scared.

We all looked at the man. And he looked at us. He was sitting on the floor in a sleeping bag. There was a little rucksack beside where he had been lying but nothing else. He had a very pale face, and he looked like he hadn't shaved for several days. He smiled and said, "Hello."

Terry said, "We didn't mean no harm, Mister."

I said, "We didn't know there was any-body here, honest."

The man licked his lips. He said, "It's all right. I'm a friend."

Lucy said, "Please can we go then, please?"

The man just looked from one to another of us for a bit. He looked scared himself. He put a hand up to his face and closed his eyes and said, "Oh God," as though everything was going wrong. Then he looked at us again. I didn't move. Neither did any of the others. We were all too scared. I hardly even breathed. It was like playing statues, like you do at parties, and the man was the per-son watching to decide who was to be out. He kept licking his lips, as though they kept going dry. Then he sort of groaned and looked really sorry for himself and said, "Oh hell, I wish you hadn't come up here." I wished we hadn't gone up there too. "What am I going to do now?" he said. He kept looking from one to the other of us as if he was wanting one of us to tell him.

He said, "Look, I'm in trouble. I need help. Will you be my friends?"

26

Nobody said anything. I could hear the crane engine and the sound of stones hitting the ground and the men's voices calling to each other on the far side of the canal. I wondered if they would hear us if we called for help from the window—and what the man would do if we did.

He looked really worried. "I'm a friend," he said. "Honest. I won't hurt you. I really am in trouble." He stared hard at each of us as if he was trying to see from our faces who would be most likely to help him. He looked back to me. Straight into my eyes.

"Will you help me?" he said.

It was the way he looked into my eyes. When someone's going to hurt you, even a teacher, they can't look at you like that. And he said it as though he knew I would help him. As though he'd picked me out especially. And I felt pleased and not so scared then. But I was still a bit scared. I looked at the others. We were all standing close together right up against the wall by the window, as far away from the man as we could get. Christine and Terry were both staring at the man with frightened faces, but Lucy looked at me and nodded.

Then I said, "Yeah." My voice was shaking. "I'll help you."

He looked a bit relieved. "That's great," he said. "Well, sit down. Go on." He made a gesture around the room with his hand as though he was in a proper house with furniture and everything. "Sit down and I'll tell you all about it. Do you want to hear? I'll *confide* in you." He made it sound like confiding was something really special and grown-up. But none of us moved. We all just went on standing there like statues. Nobody sat down. There was only the dirty old floor to sit on anyway. He held his hands out to us and kind of shrugged.

"Please. Come on. If we're going to be friends. Sit down. Shake hands." He held a hand out to each of us in turn but still nobody moved. "Look," he said, "I'll tell you what. How about a pipe of peace? Will you smoke a pipe of peace with me? Do you smoke, any of you?"

Terry said, "Yeah, I do." He didn't really.

Well, you know, he had a puff sometimes like everybody does, but he couldn't smoke like a grown-up.

The man said, "Well, look. Pass me my rucksack. We'll have to do it properly. I haven't got a pipe but I've got some cigarettes. They'll do just as good. We'll have a cigarette."

His orange rucksack was over beside where he'd been before he'd slid across to the doorway. Lucy went over and got it for him and then came back to us. The man opened the rucksack and fished around inside. He brought out a squashed-looking pack of cigarettes and a box of matches and then looked in again. "Oh yes," he said. He brought out a half package of crackers. He took all the crackers out of the package and put them in his lap. He glanced at us, counting. He put out five crackers in a row, then broke the remaining two in half and put the halves on top of four of the crackers. Then he opened the cigarettes. "Oh damn," he said. "Only one left." He brushed the crumbs off his hands and put the bent cigarette to his lips. "Here y'are." He held out one lot of crackers. "Here y'are," he said again. Terry went over and took them. He's always the first to grab anything that's going for free. "Don't eat them yet," the man said. Then he held out the next lot and Lucy and I both started forward, but I got them. Then Lucy. He held out the crackers to Christine.

"No thank you," she said.

"I'll have hers," said Terry.

"Well, hang on," said the man. "Are you sure?" he said to Chris.

"Well all right," she said. I think she only took them just so Terry couldn't have them.

"O.K. All sit down," said the man. He was smiling but looking worried at the same time. "There any more kids about?" he said, and his smile went away.

"No," said Lucy. It scared me more when his smile went away.

"There's only us," I said.

"Right," he said, and he nodded and his worried smile came back. "Sit down. Sit down." We moved closer and sat down on the floor facing him. Christine took a piece of wallpaper that had peeled off and cleaned a place for herself to sit.

"First," he said, "we have to smoke a pipe of peace. We have to pass the pipe of peace around. This cigarette will be the pipe of peace. Once we smoke the pipe of peace together, that means we mustn't ever betray each other. Right? Then we'll share this food. Breaking bread together means that we'll always take care of one another and help one another. O.K.? Now!" He lit the cigarette with a match. He swallowed the smoke.

Then he passed the cigarette to Christine, who was the first. She had to kneel up to reach it off him. She took a little suck and blew the smoke away and made a face. The man motioned her to pass it to me. I tried to suck some smoke in but it burnt my throat and I started coughing. I tried to blow the smoke out again but it went up my nose and made my eyes water. Then Lucy took it. She pretended to do it but she only held the smoke in her mouth. You could see. Then Terry. He swallowed the smoke. He was showing off. Then Terry went and gave it back and came and sat down again.

The man took another drag and then he pinched the cigarette out between his fingers. He must have had really strong fingers because it didn't hurt him at all. He put the cigarette back into the pack and smiled at us.

"Come closer," he said. "Come on. I haven't got the Black Death or anything. Don't sit way over there." Lucy moved nearer to the man, so me and Terry shuffled a bit closer as well. The man said, "That's good. That's good. Right. Now, let's share our bread." He meant the crackers. He started to eat his so we all ate ours. Terry stuffed the whole of his in his mouth at once and made himself look like a monkey. The crackers had gone all soft and weren't crunchy anymore. When the man finished eating he said, "That's good," again, and nodded his head.

"My name's Dave," he said. He looked at Terry. "What's yours?"

"Terry Jarvis." Terry mumbled it quiet like he did in school when a teacher asked his name when he was in trouble.

"What?"

"Terry Jarvis."

"Eh?" The man turned his head to the side like a bird, and cupped his hand to his ear.

"His name's Terry Jarvis," Lucy said.

"No, let him tell me," he said.

"Terry Jarvis," said Terry.

"Oh, Terry. Good. That's a good name. And you?"

"Lucy Collins."

"Lucy. Beautiful. I like that name. If I ever get married and have a little girl, I think I'll call her Lucy."

Lucy smiled. I could see she was trying not to, but she couldn't help it because she was so pleased.

"You?"

"Andy," I said.

"Andy. Great. I had a friend called Andy when I was at school. He was a good mate." He looked at Christine and smiled and raised his eyebrows.

"Christine," she said. "He's my brother."

"Yeah?" said the man. "That's good. You don't look like each other."

34

"That's 'cause she's not really my sister," I said.

He looked puzzled. Christine said quietly, "Shut up!"

"It don't matter," I said to her. Then to the man, "I mean we're sort of . . . We live with her mum and my dad."

"Oh," he said. "Oh, I see." He nodded his head. "I didn't used to live with my mum and dad when I was a kid. I lived with my gran." He smiled at me and Christine and then he said, "Right. Now, Christine, Andy, Lucy, Terry, we're bound now, like blood brothers and sisters. We've smoked the pipe of peace together. That means we'll never betray one another. And we've broken bread together. That means we'll always help one another. Right?" He held his hand out toward Lucy and Lucy edged a bit more forward and shook his hand. Then he shook hands with me and Terry, and then Christine had to move closer to shake hands with him. She cleaned another place for herself with her bit of wallpaper. She's funny like that. The man—Dave—didn't get up at all. He just sat where he was with his legs inside his sleeping bag. I wondered if he was an invalid or something who didn't have proper legs. When Christine had sat down and we were all in a close half circle around him he said, "When I told you I was in trouble and needed help I really meant it. Do you want to hear about it?"

"Yeah," said Lucy. She didn't seem at all scared anymore. I still was a bit. But not much. The look on his face and the way he spoke made it seem like he really did need our help. And that made me feel O.K.

"I'm on the run," he said. "From the police and the army."

Lucy said, "Wow. Have you robbed a bank?"

"No," said Dave. "I haven't robbed anything. See, I was out of work for a long time. I couldn't get a job. And I had nowhere proper to live after my gran died. So what I did, I joined the army. I've been in the army a couple of years. And then at the end of last year they sent me to Northern Ireland."

"What did they send you there for?" Terry said.

" 'Cause that's where the war is, dopey," I said.

"It's not a war," Christine said. She always thinks she knows everything.

"Yes it is a war," I said. "Otherwise they wouldn't be killing each other, would they?"

"There's always bombs going off and people shooting each other in the street," Lucy said. "It's on the news on television every night."

"That's not a war," said Christine. "If there was a war there'd be planes dropping bombs and everything."

"It is a war, isn't it, Dave?" I said.

"Well, it's a sort of war," he said. "It's not like the world war. I mean it's not like two big armies fighting each other. There's two lots of people there, and one lot is better off than the other, like white people and black people in South Africa. And they've been fighting among themselves. Then the army was sent there to try and put things back as they were."

"Then why aren't you in Ireland now?" Lucy said.

"Well, I've been on leave. But I was supposed to go back." He shook his head. "I don't know," he said. Then he looked at us. "Do you think I ought to go back?"

I looked at the others. I didn't know either. I didn't know what to say. It was like when a teacher asked you a question in school. I just shrugged.

Christine said, "I don't know. It depends if you're supposed to be there. I mean, if you're a soldier, you have to do what you're told, don't you?"

"If there was a dog in your street," Dave said, "and the man next door told you to go and kick it, would you do it?"

Nobody said anything.

Dave said, "Would you, Christine?"

"Would you kick Spotty Sally?" I asked. She ignored me. "No," she said to Dave.

"Suppose it was your dad who told you," Dave said.

"My dad wouldn't tell me to do that," she said.

"But just suppose he did," said Dave. "Would you?"

"No," she said.

"But you're supposed to do what your dad says, aren't you?"

Dave looked at me. I looked down at the dirty old floorboards. A tiny spider came running across the floor toward me and disappeared down a crack between two boards.

"What about you, Andy?" he said. I jumped when he said my name. "When you grow up, if you go into the army, and the army tells you you've got to go and kill Terry, would you do that?"

"Course not," I said.

"Well, if the army says you've got to, what will you do?"

"I'll go and tell him so he can get away."

"But you might not be able to. They might bring him in as a prisoner and say he's a deserter and order you to shoot him."

I looked at Terry. He was biting his fingernails. "I wouldn't be a deserter," he said.

"Anyway, I wouldn't do it," I said. "Even if they told me to."

"But then they'd put you in prison."

"Then I'd escape," I said.

"But I don't want to go to prison," Dave said. "I might not be able to escape. And I'd be old when I came out."

I looked at Dave and tried to imagine him being very old, but I couldn't. I wondered what it would be like to be in prison. And I thought that living on your own in this dirty little room with the plaster falling off the wall was a bit like being in prison. And I knew that I didn't ever want to go to prison either.

"Is that why you're running away?" said Christine.

"Yeah," said Dave. "I don't want to go to prison. But I don't want to go back to Ireland. Do you know why the soldiers are in Ireland?"

"No," said Lucy.

"Not really," said Christine. She was drawing patterns in the dirt on the floor with her fingertip and then smoothing them out again.

"No, well, I don't either," said Dave. "I couldn't understand it. But I know one thing. The people who live there don't want us there. None of them. That was plain. They were always shouting at us. Telling us to go home. Calling us names. If Irish soldiers came here and put your dads in prison and smashed up all your furniture, I expect you'd call them names, wouldn't you?"

"Is that what you did?" Christine asked. "Smashed up people's furniture?"

"Yeah. We had to. We had to search people's houses to see if they had any guns. They could of hidden them anywhere. We had to pull the kiddies out of bed and rip up the mattresses to see if there was anything inside. We had to take up the floorboards and pull the fireplaces off the walls. Tear the stuffing out of chairs. Everything." While he was talking Dave was pulling and tearing with his hands as though he had invisible mattresses and things there in his lap, and his face looked really upset as if it was disgusted with what his hands were doing. He waited for a bit and then started

41

to say something else and then stopped again, as if he couldn't decide whether to say it or not. He took a deep breath.

"One day a little kid ran up and threw a firecracker at us. It landed just behind my mate. My mate jumped around. He thought it was a shot. He thought someone was shooting at us. The little kid was running away and as my mate jumped around he fired and hit the kid. He was just a little boy. He fell in the road. He was dead. We had to say he was throwing a bomb."

I stared at Dave. He wasn't looking at us. His face had gone all white, and he was looking down and twisting his fingers together and frowning. You could tell it was the truth, what he said, because he looked as if he was going to cry. He sniffed and looked up at us.

Terry said, "Last fireworks time, me and Andy did that, didn't we, Andy. We chucked firecrackers behind people to make them jump."

Dave groaned. He said, "Yeah, it's little kids like you who get killed in Ireland." He closed his eyes and pressed a hand over them and just stayed sitting like that. Christine finished another pattern in the dirt and rubbed it out.

"What about them people who put bombs in English pubs?" she said. "They're Irish."

"Well you know why they do that, don't you," Dave said. "They want the English soldiers to get out of Ireland. If we got out of Ireland, they'd stop putting bombs in England."

"Then why don't we get out?" I asked.

"I don't know," said Dave. "That's what I can't understand. All I know is I don't want to go back there. But I don't want to go to prison either."

"I don't want you to go to prison," I said.

"Nor do I," said Lucy.

"Well then, will you make me a promise?" said Dave. "Will you promise me you won't tell anybody I'm here? Not even your best friends. Not even your mums and dads."

"I won't tell anybody," I said.

"We're blood brothers and sisters," said Lucy. "We can't betray you now."

"You see, there's something else," said Dave. "I'm sorry I frightened you at first. I would of just gone away and hid somewhere else, but I can't walk. See, the police came after me at my friend's house, but I got away."

"And you've been shot in the leg," said Lucy.

"No, no, nothing like that. It was just that it was dark when I came to the canal. I was climbing over the wall and it started crumbling and I fell and twisted my ankle. I don't know if it's broken or not, but it's all swelled up." He pulled his leg up out of the sleeping bag with his hands, and his face grimaced with pain. He showed us his ankle. It was all swollen. Huge. Soft like a balloon when it's lost some of its air. "I can't get my shoe on," he said. "And I can't walk on it. I'll have to stay here till it gets better."

It was funny—when I'd first heard him move behind us and I'd looked around, he'd seemed like a great big reptile sort of monster slithering along the ground that was going to kill us or something. But when I looked at him now he seemed small and sad, and I didn't feel scared anymore. I wanted to take care of him.

"Can we help you?" I asked.

He smiled at me. "You're helping me already," he said. "But just don't let anyone else know I'm here. Please."

"What about food?" said Christine. "Have you got anything to eat?"

"Well, no. Not now. They were the last of the crackers. But the faucet's still working downstairs, so I'll be all right for a bit. You can live without food, but you can't live without water."

"We can get you some food," I said. "We can smuggle you some."

"No, that's all right," he said quickly. "Better not do that."

"Well you can't not have any food," said Christine.

"I can get you something off my mum," said Lucy.

"No, no," said Dave. "No. Honest. I'll be all right. See, supposing your mum asked what it was for."

"I'll take it when she's not looking," Lucy said.

"Yeah, but she might notice it's gone. Listen, if anyone finds out I'm here, I'll be in dead trouble. You mustn't do anything, or say anything, to let on I'm here. O.K.? Promise?"

"But we can get you something without anyone knowing," I said. "Honest we can."

"Well, if you can . . ." Dave said very slowly. "The only thing is, be careful. Don't let anybody get suspicious, will you. I'd rather not have anything than get anybody suspicious."

Later when we got outside and away from the house, Terry said, "Shall we call the police?"

I said, "What for?"

Christine said, "Don't you dare, Terry Jarvis, or else!"

"Or else what?" he said.

"Or else I'll do you."

"You and whose army?" he said.

"Her and me," I said.

"And me," said Lucy. "We're all supposed to be blood brothers and sisters."

"You took his crackers," Christine said.

"That wasn't crackers," Lucy said. "That was bread. We shared his bread."

"Well all right, bread then. But he took it and ate it, didn't he?"

"Yeah, and you smoked a pipe of peace," I said. "That means you mustn't ever betray him."

"All right, all right," Terry said. "I only asked."

"Well it was a rotten mean thing to even think of," said Christine.

"All right, keep your hair on," said Terry.

"Well, are you his friend or aren't you?" she asked.

"I never said I wasn't, did I?"

"Well if you're his friend, then you wouldn't tell the police," said Lucy.

"I didn't say I was going to tell."

We all stopped walking and Christine shoved Terry back against the wall and held him there with her hands pressed on his chest. Me and Lucy got hold of his arms. Christine said, "Do you promise not to tell a living soul about Dave?"

Terry was scared. I could see it in his eyes. "Of course I do," he said.

"Say, on your mother's deathbed," said Lucy.

"On my mother's deathbed," said Terry. "Cross my heart and hope to die."

THREE

Every day that week Christine and me and Lucy pinched some food. Whatever we could get. We used to slip stuff into little bags in our pockets during meals when nobody was looking. We took stuff out of the pantry when Mum was out. We didn't spend our pocket money on sweets, or go to the Saturday-morning movies, or even get our comics that were ordered every week. We didn't tell Dave, but we put all our money together and went to a shop—not the one in our street, in case anybody who knew us saw us, but another one—and bought food with it. We took him the papers from the day before. Christine's got her own radio—Mum and Dad gave it to her for Christmas—she lent him that.

The first day, we lugged an old mattress up to Dave's room from the house next door, because Dave said he was getting sore from sleeping on the boards. And we got some old cushions for us to sit on, and a box for Dave to use. We stood it on end and the inside made a cupboard and the top made a table.

The third time, there was only me and Lucy there. Christine had had to go out with Mum to buy some shoes for school. I'd called for Terry but he was in trouble and his mum wouldn't let him out. She's really horrible to him half the time. She's always hitting him and his sisters. She hits them with coat hangers. His dad gives them the strap. I'd hate to live at their house. Anyway me and Lucy took Dave his dinner. We got him a tin of sardines and what was left of a loaf of bread, and a bottle of milk. Dave said he was afraid some other kids might just come into the house like we did. "They might not be such brave people as you," he said. "They might call the police."

"What can we do?" Lucy said.

"I don't know," Dave said. "Is there some way we could board the place up?"

"We come in through the cellar," she said.

"Yeah, so did I," said Dave.

"We could block that up easy," I said.

"Then how would we get in and out, dopey?" said Lucy.

"We could have a secret way of opening it," I said.

Dave took a swig of milk, and then offered the bottle to me and Lucy, but we both shook our heads. Lucy doesn't even like milk anyway, and I didn't want to take his. He put the milk bottle down on the floor beside his sleeping bag and slowly opened the sardine can with the key. He must of been hungry because we couldn't bring him much. Not even as much as I ate. But he never said anything about it. And he didn't gobble the food fast or anything.

"What about another way?" he said. "What about finding another way for you to come in and out?"

"There aren't any other ways," said

Lucy. "Through the cellar's the only way."

We were sitting on the end of Dave's mattress facing the window. "We could climb in the window," I said.

"Don't be daft," she said. "How could we?"

I got up and went over to the window, and Lucy followed me. We looked down to the ground. It seemed a long way down.

"Is there anything you could climb up?" said Dave.

"What about a ladder?" Lucy said.

"We haven't got a ladder," I said.

"Well we can get one," she said.

"Where from?"

"I don't know."

"And how?"

"We can steal one."

"Maybe that's not a good idea," said Dave. "What else could we use instead of a ladder?"

"A rope," I said. "What about a rope?"

"Yeah," said Lucy. "I'm good on ropes in the gym."

"My dad's got a rope," I said. "In the car. He found it on the motorway."

"Oh great," said Lucy.

"It was one that fell off the back of a truck," I said.

Dave laughed. "I've heard about things like that before," he said.

"It really did," I said. "My dad saw it on the motorway and he stopped on the side and ran back to get it. He said it'd come in useful. He says you never know when you'll need a bit of rope."

"He was right too," said Dave. His mouth was full of sardines.

"We're always needing ropes," I said. " 'Cause our car's always breaking down and we have to get it towed."

Dave took a piece of bread and folded it and wiped it around and around the inside of the sardine tin until it was as shiny and clean as if Spotty Sally had been licking it. "Can you get it without anybody noticing?" he asked.

"Yeah," I said. "I can get it tonight. After my dad gets home from work."

So that evening Christine and me called for Lucy and Terry after supper and took the rope to the house. We went in through the cellar same as usual and went up to Dave's room.

"Hello," he said. "It's lovely to see your smiling faces."

"I've got the rope," I said. It was quite a long one, and heavy to carry. I felt proud to have brought it, but I was glad to be able to drop it on the floor. It made the plaster dust rise up in a cloud.

"Oh Andy!" Christine said. "What did you do that for?"

"Never mind," said Dave. He started to cough. The dust made him cough and I was sorry I'd done it, and felt silly. "It looks like a great rope," he said when he stopped coughing, and he smiled at me and I felt O.K. again. "Right," he said. "After tea we'll get to work."

"We haven't got much food," Christine said. She gave him half a package of biscuits and Lucy gave him four eggs.

"They're raw," she said. "I don't know how we can cook them."

"Never mind about that," said Dave. "Give 'em here."

He took one egg and banged it on the top

of Lucy's head. Then he tipped his own head back and pulled the eggshell in half so that the raw egg slid into his mouth. He chewed a couple of times, then swallowed, and then grinned at us and rolled his eyes.

"Eugh!" said Terry.

"Oh Dave!" said Christine. "How could you!"

Lucy just stared at him with her mouth open.

"Do it again," I said.

"Too right I will," he said. "Come here, egghead."

I went to him and knelt down and he cracked the next one on my head.

"Come on, Terry," he said. "It gives them a flavor." And he did it to Terry. When it was Christine's turn she wouldn't let him do it on her head.

"I don't want all egg in my hair," she said.

"What are you talking about?" he said. "There's no egg in their hair. Look. And anyway, egg shampoo's great for your hair." And he cracked the last one on his own head.

Me and Terry and Lucy went down to the cellar. There was lots of junk in the house. We jammed an old door up against the coal hole with a bedstead and pieces of wood and stuff. Like a barricade. It was difficult to do because it was completely dark once the opening was boarded up. We had to do it all by feel. Everything was dirty and damp and smelly, but it didn't matter because what we had to do was important to keep Dave safe.

When we went back upstairs Christine was sitting beside Dave and he had his arm around her. She looked as if she'd been crying.

"We've done it, Dave," I said.

"No one'll get in there now," Terry said. "We've made sure of that."

"Great!" said Dave. "I feel safer now."

"What about the rope now?" I said.

"Hang about a bit," he said. "Me and Christine are having a chat. We'll do it in a minute."

"That's all right," she said. "We can't talk anymore now they're here."

"Sure we can," said Dave. "We're all

blood brothers and sisters, aren't we?"

"Yeah," she said. "But I don't want to."

"O.K.," said Dave. "Let's see about this rope then. Is there a floorboard loose over there we could pry up?"

"They're all loose," Terry said.

"O.K.," said Dave. "Let's pull one up that's about level with the middle of the window."

"This one?" said Terry.

"Yeah, that'll do."

It came up dead easy. Dave slid across the room in his sleeping bag, making a trail in the dirt like a boat through the water. He looked down at the beam showing under the floor.

"Here, Terry," he said. "Stick your foot through that plaster, will you?"

Terry put his foot down the hole and stamped on the ceiling of the room underneath till some plaster broke away and fell with a *crump* on the floor downstairs.

"That'll do it," said Dave. He took the end of the rope and passed it around the beam and began knotting it. "Sorry to hear about you being in trouble this afternoon,

Terry," he said. "What was all that about?"

"Oh, nothing," he said. "I beat up my sister."

"Is that why your mum wouldn't let you out?"

"Well, my sister went crying to my mum when she was cooking the dinner, so she hit me with the fish slicer. So I swore at her, so she locked me in the cupboard under the stairs." Terry was standing by the hole in the floor. One of his baseball boots didn't have a lace in—the one he'd stamped the ceiling in with—and it had flakes of white plaster on it. He'd tied it with a piece of string. Dave was sitting at his feet. He looked up into Terry's face and shook his head.

"She shouldn't do that," he said.

"His dad's worse," I said. "One time when Terry got whipped at school for nothing, he told his dad, and his dad said he wouldn't get whipped for nothing. So he took his belt off and gave Terry another good hiding for whatever it was he'd done."

Dave looked as if he was going to cry. He

held his arms out to Terry, but Terry moved away.

"Oh Terry," Dave said. "What are we going to do?"

"Dunno," said Terry.

Dave shook his head. "I dunno either," he said. He sat quiet for a while.

Then Dave looked at the knot he'd made. He tried pulling at the rope as hard as he could, so that the veins stood out on his forearms. "Right," he said. "That'll hold. If we chuck this out the window, you can try climbing up and down it to make sure it's all right."

From then on, whenever we went to the house, we went around the back and whistled up to Dave. We did a special low whistle. I can do a great whistle with two fingers. Really loud. But not that. Dave said that would attract attention. We did a special quiet sort of whistle that everybody could do. Then Dave threw the rope out the window and we climbed up it.

It was quite hard to climb at first, and we grazed our knuckles on the stone wall. The next day, when me and Christine went around in the morning with some food, Dave decided to make knots all the way up the rope for hand- and footholds. Me and Christine and Dave all sat on the floor by the window while he made the knots. The sun was shining. In the sunshine, where I was sitting, it was lovely and warm. I felt really happy. When I went to see Dave it always made me feel happy and important. But Christine was looking miserable. And Dave looked sad too.

"You know what, Chris," he said. "I've been thinking about what you said yesterday."

"What?" she said. She looked a bit uncomfortable.

"It don't matter if Andy knows what we were saying, does it?" He stopped knotting for a moment and ruffled my hair with his hand. It made me feel warm when he touched me, like sitting in the sunshine.

"Well . . ." said Christine.

"You wouldn't say anything to anyone,

would you, Andy?" Dave said.

"No," I said. "Course not."

"Well don't," he said. "This is just between Christine and you and me. O.K.?"

"Yeah," I said.

"O.K., Chris?"

"Yes, all right," she said. But she didn't look very pleased about it.

"Christine was saying," Dave said to me, "about how it always seems your mum and dad like you better than her. Do you think they do?"

"No," I said. "They always treat us both the same. Except they let Christine stay up later, and give her extra things, because she's older.

"They don't," she said.

"What about your radio?" I said. "And your watch."

"Well!" she said, all angry.

"Hey listen. We're not arguing about it," Dave said. "We're just talking about a problem. To help one another. Right?"

Christine didn't say anything. I just nodded.

"See, the thing is, Chris," Dave said, "if

your mum told you she didn't like your real father, and about how he got her pregnant when she didn't want him to, and how she didn't want you before you were born and when you were just a little baby—well, she could only tell you those things because she loves you now."

"S'pose so," Christine said.

"Well of course," Dave said. "Look, when my mum used to come to see me at my gran's house, she didn't ever say anything like that to me. She always pretended she really wanted me. But if she had, she'd of taken me with her, wouldn't she? Or at least she'd of come more than twice a year."

"Did she only used to come twice a year?" Christine said. She was making patterns in the dirt again. Whenever she sat on the floor in Dave's room, she always made patterns in the dirt. Her schoolbooks were always covered in patterns. She was always getting in trouble for it at school—although I don't know why because they were great patterns. I wish I could do patterns like her.

"Yeah," Dave said. "When I was small she used to come on my birthday and at

Christmas. Till she stopped coming at all. But what I mean is, because she didn't want me, she couldn't tell me she hadn't wanted me when I was a baby. Do you see? Your mum can only tell you now, Chris, because she grew to love you and want you so *much*."

"Mum and Dad do love you, Chris," I said.

"I know," she said. But her lips quivered, and she started to cry. Dave stopped knotting the rope.

"Come here," he said. And he patted the floor beside him. Christine climbed over his legs and sat close up to him without even cleaning the floor first. Dave cuddled her.

"I s'pose," he said, "babies understand more than people think. I expect, when you were tiny, you sensed she didn't want you. Maybe the way she held you, or fed you, or something. And that's why you get the feeling now."

Christine just cried. Dave beckoned me, and I moved closer and he cuddled me as well. I put one arm around him and one around Christine.

"You know what?" Dave said. "I think you two are real lovely kids. And you wouldn't be like that if your mum and dad didn't love you."

"But he's not my real dad," Christine said. "And mum and dad aren't married, and they've got different names so everyone knows he isn't my real dad. I just wish I had a real mum and dad of my own."

"Yeah, I suppose that's what we all need," Dave said. "But I think it's better to have a mum and dad like you've got than to have a real mum and dad like Terry's."

"Oh yeah," said Christine.

"I wouldn't swap our mum and dad for anyone," I said. "I think they're great." Then I thought about it. "Most of the time," I said.

One day Spotty Sally followed us to the house. We'd all climbed up the rope into the room and left her, so she started barking and whining. Dave was worried she was going to attract attention. We shouted down at her in loud whispers to go home, but she wouldn't. And none of us wanted to have to be the one to take her. In the end I went down the rope, and she stopped barking and came with me around to the front of the house. Lucy went down to the cellar and made a small opening in the barricade over the coal chute. Sally wriggled through that. Dogs can get through really small holes that you'd think only a cat could get through.

By the time I climbed back up the rope, Sally was in the doorway growling at Dave. All the hair along her back was standing up. She was trying to make herself look bigger. Her head was down close to the floor. Her ears lay back flat on her head and her tail was curled under between her legs. Her lips were curled back showing all her white teeth.

Lucy knelt down and rubbed her cheek on the fur of Sally's head and hugged her. "It's all right, Sal," she said. "It's only Dave."

I went to Dave. "Come on, Spot," I said. "He's a friend. Come on. Give him a kiss."

Spotty Sally came over barking at Dave,

but she began wagging her tail at the same time. "It's all right," I said to Dave. "She's wagging her tail now. She's just barking 'cause that's the only way she can talk." I knelt down and put my arms around Dave to show Sally he was a friend. Sally licked his face.

"Hello Spotty Sally," Dave said, wiping the lick off. "You're a very nice dog." Sal barked at him and licked him again. And then she licked me, and then went and licked Lucy and Christine and Terry, one after the other. Terry was sitting on a cushion biting his nails. Christine was unpacking the food we'd brought onto Dave's table. Lucy came and knelt down with me and Dave on the mattress.

"Sal's great," Lucy said.

"But she can look real fierce," Dave said. "I thought you were very brave, Luce, to cuddle her when she was growling."

"She was just looking after us," Lucy said. "I used to be scared of dogs. A dog bit me once. But since Spotty Sally's been in our gang, I'm not scared anymore."

"That's good," Dave said. "I think dogs

only bite you if you're scared of them."

"Yeah, that's right," she said. "They never bite me anymore."

Me and Lucy both sat down on the mattress.

"Hey," Dave said, "mind my foot."

"Be careful," Christine said, all bossy. "Let Dave eat his dinner."

"It's O.K., Chris," he said. "I'll get into that in a minute."

Spotty Sally was standing with her front feet on the sill, and her ears straight up, looking out of the window. The mill was all knocked down by then. There was a bulldozer working at pushing all the stones and rubble into mounds, and some men were making a huge bonfire of all the old wood.

"Why do you call her Spotty Sally?" Dave said. He took a lump of cheese off his table and bit into it. "She's not spotty, she's black."

"She's not," said Lucy proudly. "She's got two brown spots over her eyes."

"When they gave her to the little girl next door, they told her to choose a name," said Christine. "And she said 'Spotty Sally' because she's got those spots."

I said, "My dad says the spots are there to help the dog fight rats. The rats go for dogs' eyes, and those light brown spots look like eyes, so the rats bite the wrong place."

Sally got down from the window and came and stood on Dave's sleeping bag. She turned around in a circle about three times, and then she slumped down and curled up against Dave's legs. She sighed and put her nose between her front paws.

"She's your friend now, Dave," I said.

"That's good," he said. "I need all the friends I can get."

We went to the house every day that week, and spent a lot of time there. Dave talked to us a lot. He'd been all over in the army. He'd even been in Germany.

"What was it like in Germany, Dave?" I asked him.

"Did you kill lots of Krauts?" Terry said.

"No," said Dave. He said it sharp, like cracking a whip. "I didn't kill anyone in Germany."

It upset me when his voice was hard like that. His face had gone hard too. I wanted the hardness to go.

"Did you like Germany?" I said.

"Yeah," he said. "It was great." But he still didn't smile. "There was no fighting there."

"What do you do in the army if there's no fighting, Dave?" asked Lucy.

"Oh they're never short of ideas in the army for dumb things to make you do."

"I thought you said you liked it there," said Christine.

"I did," he said. "I really did. I mean, the army's only a job. Any job, you have to do things you don't like, don't you. Like in a car factory, or anything. You only do it for the money. But it's like you just deaden yourself at work. It's after work when you're living. I had a good time in Germany."

"What doing?" I said.

Dave looked down at the sleeping bag, and smiled to himself. The sleeping bag was covered with white from the plaster dust on the floor. "I had a girl friend there," he said.

"What was she like?" asked Christine.

Dave looked at Christine and smiled. "She was great," he said. "She was the nicest girl I ever met, before I met you and Lucy."

"No, but what was she like, really?" said Christine. She knelt down in front of him. Lucy went and sat on the sleeping bag and looked up at Dave, and he put his arm around her. Terry and me were sitting on the windowsill. Terry coughed and spat out the window. He wanted to show that he thought talking about girls was soft.

Dave said, "She was older than me. And she was so nice. It was funny because I couldn't speak much German, and she couldn't speak English very well, but we always understood each other. She understood me better than any of the guys in the army. We felt the same about things."

"Was she pretty?" Christine said.

"Well, not like a model or a film star or anything. But she had a lovely face. You could see how kind she was in her face."

"Why didn't you marry her?" said Lucy.

"I would of done," he said. "But she was married already."

"How could she be your girl friend if she was married?" Lucy said.

"It don't make any difference," I said. "Someone's your girl friend if you love them. You can't help it if they're married or not."

"Did you love her, Dave?" said Christine.

"Yeah," he said. "Still do."

"Why didn't you run away with her?" said Lucy.

"I would of done. But she had two kids. A little boy and a little girl."

"You should of brought them," I said. "You'd of been a great dad."

"I wish I could of," he said. "I wish I could of." He was stroking Lucy's hair with one hand. Gently stroking it over the side of her face, without thinking what he was doing. I wished it was me he was stroking, but I didn't say anything. Terry would of laughed at me.

"We thought about it. But her husband wouldn't let the kids leave the country. He didn't care about them at all. He just wanted them like possessions. He wouldn't let them go. And the army wouldn't let me stay. So I haven't seen her for a long time. I think about her a lot though. Think about her all the time."

"What was her name?" Christine said.

"Vikki."

"I wish she was here now," Lucy said.

"So do I," said Dave, and he smiled a sad smile to himself.

I wished she was there too. Christine and Lucy both hugged Dave. And then I went and hugged him too. I didn't care what Terry thought.

One time when we went to Dave's, me and Terry nearly had a fight. Terry, Lucy, and me were walking on top of the wall around the old closed-down school. Christine thinks she's too grown-up to walk on walls, so she just walked on the pavement. When we came to the gateway, Terry jumped across. It's really wide and you had to land and balance on the wall on the other

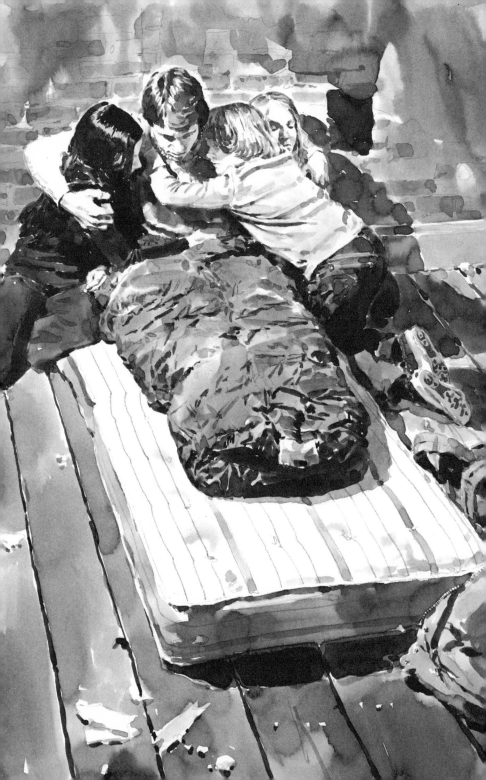

side. I wouldn't jump. Terry kept saying "Go on. 'S easy. 'S kid stuff." And Lucy kept pushing me in the back every time I was just going to jump. Then Christine got all bad-tempered about it and kept saying, "Oh come on, will you." So in the end I climbed down. Then Lucy jumped the gap and made it, and they all laughed at me. They kept on about it, especially Terry, all the way, and even after we got to Dave's. I didn't like them going on at me at all, but when we got to Dave's it was even worse because I didn't want him to know I'd been scared. Terry kept jabbing me with his fingers and chanting, "Andy's a chicken. Andy's a chicken."

He said to Dave, "He couldn't even jump a gap in the wall."

I said, "Well Lucy was pushing me in the back all the time, wasn't she."

Dave said, "I'm not so hot at jumping off walls. Look what I did last time I tried." He was talking about his ankle.

"Yeah, but it wasn't a wall like that," Terry said. "It was just a gap where the gate was. Even Lucy jumped it."

"Well nobody was pushing her," I said.

"What d'you mean, *even* Lucy?" Dave asked. "I bet Lucy's a great jumper."

"Yeah, but she's a girl," Terry said.

"Well I had a girl friend at school," Dave said, "who was the school long-jump champion. She even won the East London schools championships. And she could run faster than me and all."

"Yeah, but he's still chicken," Terry said, poking me again.

"Shut up, Big Head. I'm not chicken," I said.

"Then why didn't you jump then?" he sneered in a singsong voice.

"Because I didn't want to. So there."

"You were scared. You're a scaredy-cat."

"No I'm not. I just didn't want to, that's all. And I've seen you crying because you were scared."

"No you haven't."

"Oh yes I have."

"When?"

"When Tom Caton was after you for kicking his little sister."

"I was not."

"Oh yes you were."

"No I wasn't." He said it through gritted teeth, and thumped me on my arm muscle so my arm went paralyzed. I pushed him away and he thumped my arm again. "Come on," he said. "Wanna fight?"

I said, "No. I don't want to fight."

"Because you're scared," he said.

"Oh stop it, you two," Christine said. "Just stop it." Terry thumped my arm again. "Dave, tell them to stop it," Christine said. "It's stupid."

"It does seem dumb fighting your friends," Dave said.

"That's why I don't want to fight," I said. But they all knew I was scared. I was scared because Terry is a better fighter than me. Last time we had a fight he gave me a nose-bleed.

Dave said, "Come on and sit down with me, you fellers." I went and sat next to him and he put his arm around me. Terry wouldn't come even though Dave held his arm out to him. Terry sat down with his back against the wall.

"I don't like seeing my friends fighting

among themselves," Dave said. "And being scared's nothing to be ashamed of." I had to bite my bottom lip. Otherwise I would of cried. "If you only knew all the things I'm scared of," he said. "I'm even scared of the dark."

"I used to be scared of the dark," said Lucy.

"Well I still am," said Dave.

I thought about him being there in the empty house, on his own in the dark, every night when we were home in bed. I would of been scared. But I hadn't known Dave was.

"I'm scared in the day, if it comes to that," he said. "When you're not here. Scared someone'll come. That they'll find me. Cart me off to the army prison. Prison guards are bad enough, but they're even worse in *army* prisons. They really treat you like subhumans there. But it's even more scary at night. The dark. The noises. Rats and mice. I was scared in Ireland too. Scared I was going to get shot. Being scared's nothing to be ashamed of. If you're scared of a bully who's bigger than you, that's common sense, isn't it? You're scared of him because you know he can hurt you. So the best thing is to run away. And if you're scared of spiders—well there's not much sense in that I suppose, because spiders can't hurt you."

"Christine's scared of spiders," Terry said.

Christine turned on him. "So!" she said.

"Well, if you're scared of them, you're scared of them," Dave said. "You can tell yourself there's nothing to be afraid of, dark or spiders can't hurt you. But if you're still frightened anyway—well there's nothing you can do about it. It don't matter. But the important thing is this." Dave turned his head to look at me, still holding me tight with his arm around me. "If you're scared of that bully, and he says he'll thump you if you don't tell him where your mate's hiding, what are you going to do?"

I looked away from Dave's face and down at the little mountain range of rubble along by the wall made by the plaster that had fallen off. I wondered whether I would give Dave away if I was being bullied. I thought about Tom Caton and his big hard fists. I remembered when he'd beat Terry up. And afterward Tom tried to make me kick Terry, while Tom's mates held him down. Terry was crying. I wouldn't do it. Tom kept rapping my head with his knuckles till I was crying too. But I wouldn't do it.

"I'd be scared," I said. "But I wouldn't tell."

"And if they said they'd put a spider down your dress if you wouldn't tell something," Dave said to Christine, "what would you do?"

Christine shuddered. "I don't know," she said.

"I wouldn't tell, Dave," Lucy said, "no matter what they did."

"Only scaredy-cats tell," Terry said.

Dave looked at him sort of sad and shook his head slowly. "You can't help being scared," he said. "It's what you *do* when you're scared that matters."

That was the great thing about Dave. Because he was never horrible to any of us, it made me feel bad if I was being horrible. And because he liked us all, it made me like the others more. And they were nicer to me, most of the time. Dave treated me just as if I was grown up, same as he was, and that made me feel grown up. He was real nice to be with.

FOUR

It was exciting all that week. It was exciting pinching the food, in case we got caught. It was exciting going to and from the house, because we had to make sure no one saw us. It was exciting when we were there, because we had to keep watching or listening for any strangers or police coming. I used to pretend I was a secret agent all the time. I never told the others, but I think they used to pretend as well.

One day, though, I nearly got in real trouble at home. There was forty pence on the mantelpiece over our fireplace. I kept looking at it and thinking about what I could buy for Dave with it. But I didn't like to take it. First, because I didn't like stealing from my mum and dad, and second, because they might notice it was gone. I told Christine but she just said, "Go on then. Take it."

"You take it," I said.

She said, "No. I'm not going to. It was your idea."

"Well, let's do it together."

"No. You do it if you want to. Go on. They won't notice."

I kept looking at it and in the end I just took it and went to the shop.

Well, that evening, when me and Christine were clearing the table after supper, Dad said to Mum, "Here, Love, where's my change gone?"

"It's on the mantelpiece," Mum said. Christine and me looked at each other. I thought, I'm in for it now.

"No it's not," Dad said.

"You want to get yourself a pair of glasses," Mum said. "You can't see things when they're right under your nose." And she went over to the fireplace.

"Don't be silly," Dad said. "I've just looked there. I'm not that blind."

Mum shuffled bits of paper and ornaments about and moved the clock. "Well it was here," she said. "I saw it this morning."

I went into the kitchen and put the plates in the sink.

"Oh, we've got a phantom spender, have we?" Dad said.

"It's your turn to do the dishes," I whispered to Christine. "I'm going out."

"No. Wait for me," she said.

"No. 'Cause of Dad," I said.

"Here, you two," Dad called. "Have you seen my forty pence on this mantelpiece?" I froze on the spot. It was like being paralyzed. I wanted to make a run for the door, but I couldn't seem to move.

"I saw it this morning, Dad," Christine called, "but I never touched it." I glared at her. She's so sneaky sometimes.

"Andy, have you seen it, Love?" Dad said.

I swallowed and looked at Christine and then at the door.

"Andy!"

"Yes, Dad."

"Here a minute, Love."

I went into the living room.

"Have you borrowed some money off this mantelpiece?"

"Yes, Dad."

"Oh," he said. He scratched the back of his neck with his fingernail. "Well," he said, "that was mine."

I didn't say anything.

"What did you borrow it for?" he said.

I could hear Christine washing dishes in the kitchen. Mum was wiping the table top with a dishcloth. I couldn't think what to say. "What did you spend it on?" Dad said.

"Food," I said.

"Oh," he said. "Well, if you was hungry, you should of asked. Or got yourself something from the kitchen. Anyway, that was mine. I don't take your things without asking."

"You do," I said.

"No I don't."

"You do."

"When? When did I take something of yours without asking?"

"When your mate from work came with his little boy."

Dad put his hands in his pockets and pursed his lips. He glanced at Mum. I could see that she was looking at him and trying not to smile. Dad had a job not to smile as well. "Well," he said, "I thought you was being really rotten—not letting him play with anything."

"Yeah, but you still took my garage when I told you not to," I said. I felt braver because they'd nearly been smiling. But then Dad looked cross again.

"Well, I really feel ashamed," he said, "when something like that happens. A mate of mine comes here, and you behave like that. I want my friends to see what a lovely person you are. And then you go and be that selfish and horrible you won't even let a little kid play with one of your toys."

"You still took my things without asking," I said.

"Yes," he said. "You're right. I shouldn't of. If you want to be horrid, that's your lookout. Well, I'm sorry. I'll try not to do it again."

"Well, I'm sorry I took your money," I said. I thought, This is O.K. I'm going to get off light. Then he said, "Yeah, but I put it back."

"What?"

"Your thing. What I took of yours."

I didn't say anything.

"Well?"

Well, I'd spent it, hadn't I. So I couldn't put it back. I didn't know what to say.

"So you owe me forty pence," he said.

"I haven't got any money, Dad," I said.

"Well, the next forty pence you get, you give to me. Right?"

I nodded. I thought, I won't be able to help Dave much now. "Can I go out to play now?" I said.

"Yeah. Oh, hang about. Here!" He put his hand in his pocket and took out thirty pence and held it out to me. "That's 'cause you're a good mate," he said.

"Wow! Thanks, Dad," I said. I took the money and turned to run into the kitchen. I thought I'd go straight to a shop and get Dave something for supper.

"Here! Just a minute," Dad said.

I turned around in the doorway. "What?" I said.

"Wasn't there something?" he said.

"What?"

"You owe me some money," he said.

I looked at the silver coins in my hand. "What, this?" I said. I sighed and went over and gave him the thirty pence back.

"Thanks," he said. "Now you only owe me ten pence. Bye-bye. See you later."

That Sunday my dad asked me and Christine where we wanted to go for our day out.

Christine said, "I don't really want to go anywhere, Dad. Can't we stay home?"

"Stay home?" Dad said. "But it's the last chance to go out before you go back to school."

"We can go out next Sunday," Christine said.

"Yeah," said Dad. "But the summer's near enough over now, you know. We might not get much more good weather."

"We haven't got good weather now," she said.

"It's nothing to write home about," he said. "But it's all right. What about you,

Son? Do you want to go anywhere?"

I felt ever so funny when he looked at me because he had this sort of appealing hurt look in his eyes. It was as though he was the little boy, and I was the father. I said, "No thanks, Dad." And I felt horrid.

"O.K.," he said. "Please yourselves. You're a right funny pair of buggers though, I must say. When I was a kid, there's nothing I'd of liked better than to have a dad to take me out." I felt real unkind. But I couldn't help it. We were blood brothers and sisters to Dave, and we had to help him.

So we spent that Sunday with him. And the Monday. But Tuesday morning we had to go back to rotten horrible school. I felt right miserable Tuesday morning. And the others did too. Dave knew we had to go to school. We went to see him straight after. He said he'd been miserable too, on his own all day, but he felt happy when we turned up.

His ankle was still swollen and sore. It wasn't as bad as it had been at first, but it still wasn't good enough for him to be able to get away. I was pleased really, because I wanted him to stay.

We went to the house every day after school. It was usually pouring with rain. It wasn't very nice for Dave. We took him some matches and he made fires out of rubbish and wood in the little fireplace. It must have been real cold at night because there was no glass in the window. The rain used to come right into the room even though we'd put Dave's old bit of sacking back up.

Dave said it wasn't too bad because he'd got Christine's radio and that was like having a friend.

We used to go straight from school. And then we went back again after supper, most nights. There was always someone who could go. We used to save him food from our school dinners, especially Lucy, who was on dinner duty and could get seconds. Then we'd get him some more stuff from home at suppertime. But even then he was getting more ill looking.

After school on Thursday, James started to follow us. James is a right bully and a real know-all. He kept saying, "Where're you always going, you four?" And "I'm coming with yer."

"No you're not," Christine said.

"See if you can stop me," he said, and he pulled Christine's hair. She yelled. I ran up and tried to kick him in the leg, but I didn't get close enough. He let go of Christine and began to chase me. I ran as fast as I could. I was really scared. He's nearly three years older than me. I could hear his feet slap-slapping through the puddles on the gravel towpath behind me. Getting closer. I could hear his breathing. He grabbed me and threw me up against the wall, and twisted my arm up my back.

"Where're you going?" he said through gritted teeth.

I yelled. He was really hurting my arm. But I didn't say anything.

"Where're you going?" he said again, twisting my arm harder. Then Christine and Terry and Lucy came running up.

Christine said, "Leave him alone, you big bully."

He said, "Where're you going then?" He twisted my arm even more, so hard he made me cry. Then the others all started shouting and piled into him. He let go of my arm and cried out. Terry had kicked him on the shin. "I'll get you for that, Terry Jarvis," he said.

Christine shouted, "Run for it."

"Split up," yelled Lucy. And we all ran. Terry and I were running back along the towpath the way we'd come and James was running after us. I jumped for the wall and climbed on top. James ran past still chasing Terry. And gaining on him. Terry got to the footbridge. There are pipes that go across the canal under the bridge. Terry quickly shinned up a pipe, and hanging upside down from the pipe like a monkey, he clambered out over the water. James didn't dare do that. I could see Terry calling James names as he went across and James just standing on the bank threatening him. Later we all met up at Dave's.

Then on Friday something terrible happened. The first I knew of it was after lunch. I stayed at school for lunch, but Terry went home. And so did James. The first lesson afterward was arithmetic. Terry got told off for coming in late. I hate arithmetic. We'd got this horrible new teacher. We called him Sniffer, because he'd got a great red nose and he kept sniffing all the time. He was bad-tempered to everybody. But especially to Terry and me because we sat at the back, and we were always talking, and we were no good at sums. Old Sniffer wrote up all these long-division problems on the blackboard. We were supposed to be doing them on our own while he marked the compositions we'd done that morning. First we had to divide fourteen into three hundred and fifty. I could never do long division. I was going to ask Terry, even though he could never do long division either.

"Terry?"

He didn't answer. "Terry," I whispered again. He had his head turned away from me resting on his arm. I pulled his arm and he glanced around angrily and turned away again.

"Leave me alone," he said. And I saw that he was crying.

"What's the matter?" I said.

Sniffer looked up from his pile of books

all fierce like a dog when its bone's being pinched. I looked down at my book and chewed the end of my pen, trying to look as though I was thinking. Sniffer got up. I heard his chair scrape back. I thought, Oh no, he's coming to give me a clout. But his footsteps went away. I looked up and saw he'd gone over to look out the window. It had been raining on and off all the week, but just then it started to pour down in bucketsful. We'd got the lights on because the room was so dark with the clouds, and the rain was drumming very loud on the windows. We'd all have liked to go over to look out at the rain, but of course we wouldn't of been allowed. That's the trouble with teachers. They never think you'd be interested in something that they're interested in. You'd think they thought we were creatures from another planet or something. Anyway, he stood there looking out at the rain, sniffing, so I pulled Terry's sleeve again.

"What's the matter, Terry?" I said.

He looked around at me and whispered, "James knows about Dave."

"How does he know?" I said.

"I don't know. But he's going to tell his dad."

James' dad is a policeman.

"SHARPE AND JARVIS! COME OUT HERE!" I think everybody in the room must of jumped. I know I did. I nearly had a heart attack. Sniffer stomped back to his desk and leaned on it with all his fingertips. Terry sighed and tried to quickly wipe the tears from his eyes. We both got up slowly and started to walk down to the front.

"And bring your workbooks with you!" shouted Sniffer.

We both sighed again. My insides felt as though they were dropping out of me. I hate getting the stick. But I always seem to be in trouble. Terry and I got our books and took them to the front of the class. All the other kids were looking at us. Some of them were grinning at us with their faces turned away from Sniffer. They knew we were in for it.

"And be quick about it!" yelled Sniffer. But we just carried on real slow. Partly because we didn't want to get there because we were scared, and partly defiance to show him we weren't going to do anything just because he said we'd got to. We got to the front and he snatched the books away from us and laid them open in front of him on the desk. I'd written down $14 \overline{) 3 \ 5 \ 0}$ but then I'd doodled on it and changed it into a picture of a cowboy catching another man in a lasso.

Terry had got nothing on his page at all. Just a blank page. Sniffer looked at the two books for a bit. Then he said to me, "A proper little artist, then, aren't you. And what are you going to do when you grow up? If you ever do grow up. Draw pictures on the pavement? You haven't even got the talent to make a living at that." I just looked down at the floor.

"And what are you blubbering about?" he asked. I looked up, but he wasn't talking to me. He was looking at Terry. Terry bit his bottom lip, but he didn't answer. "I'm talking to you, lad!" shouted Sniffer. "I asked you what you were blubbering about!"

Terry said, "I don't know."

"You don't know! What do you mean, you don't know?"

Terry didn't say anything, so Sniffer said, "Well, I'd better give you something to cry about then, hadn't I. Hold out your hand. Both of you. Hold it up! Hold it up!"

He gave us each three with the ruler. It really stung too. But I was more sorry for Terry really, with Sniffer saying that about him blubbering in front of the whole class. And I was worrying about what would happen if James did tell his dad. So it didn't seem to hurt as bad as it does sometimes.

It had stopped raining when we came out of school. We all four went different ways, and met up under the canal bridge nearest to Dave's house. We hung around for a bit to see if anybody else came along, but no one did. So we ran down the towpath, which was all slippery and muddy and puddles everywhere, and got over the wall into the back yard. We gave the whistle. Dave whistled back and the rope came down from the window. We had a rule that the first one over the wall was first to go up the rope. Christine was first, and then Lucy. Then Terry went up, and I was last. I climbed into the room and Dave gave me a hug, like he did to everybody, and then he pulled the rope up. The others were getting the food out from pockets and bags.

"Dave," I said, "something terrible's happened."

"What?" he said.

"I'll tell him," said Terry.

"Wait a minute," said Dave. He could walk by then, but he was still limping badly. He spread out his sleeping bag and we all went to sit down on it with him. Terry sat next to him on one side, and me on the other. He put his arms around us both. Lucy and Christine knelt in front of him. "Now," he said, "let's hear this terrible news."

"James knows about you," said Terry.

"How does he know?" said Christine.

"He just does," said Terry.

"How does he just does?" she said. "How could he? You told him, didn't you?" She could make her voice sound really spiteful when she wanted. Terry started crying.

"It's all right, Terry," said Dave. And he cuddled him. He winked at Christine and said "Sshh" with his mouth. "These things happen. We've done pretty good, you know. We've been eleven days. That's a long time to keep a secret."

"You told him, didn't you, Terry?" said Christine. Dave shook his head at her.

"I couldn't help it," Terry said. "I didn't mean to."

"I'm sure you didn't," said Dave. "You're the best friends I've ever had in all my life. And I mean that." And he did mean it too. You could tell by the way he said it.

Terry said, "I'm sorry, Dave."

"It's all right, Terry."

"I didn't mean to. He just kept picking on me, and trying to make me fight, and calling me names. He said I was a coward. And I said I wasn't a coward and that I was helping a man get away from the police which was more than he would ever dare do. And I said we wouldn't let him come with us because he was a telltale-tit and no one could trust him. And I said we were all blood brothers, and that I wouldn't be a

blood brother with him for all the money in the Bank of England, and neither would you." Terry was still crying while he was talking, but when he said that Dave started to laugh.

"What did he say to that?" Dave asked.

"He just went on giving me Chinese burns and things and said I was making it up. I said I wasn't, so then he said he'd tell his dad."

"And his dad's a policeman," I said.

"What else did you say?" said Dave.

"Nothing else."

"Are you sure?"

"Nothing else. Honest."

"Does he know where I am?"

"No."

"Someone's bound to have seen us coming here if the police start asking," said Christine.

Dave nodded and thought for a minute. "Well, listen kids. My foot's not so bad now. And I'd of had to be going soon anyway. So I'd better . . ." He looked puzzled. He didn't know what to do. "I suppose I ought to go tonight really," he said.

"Where will you go?" said Lucy.

Dave smiled and shrugged. "I don't know," he said. "Maybe I should just give myself up."

"No," I said. "You mustn't do that. Don't go to prison. We'll help you."

"But I don't know where to go," he said. "And anyway, I haven't got any money."

"We'll try and get some money from somewhere," said Christine.

"Oh no," said Dave. "You mustn't do that. Now I mean it. You mustn't do that." Then he rested his face on the top of my head, and sort of nuzzled me like horses do each other. "You're great kids," he said. "I'll miss you. I really will. Still, I suppose I'd better go tonight, hadn't I?"

"But you can't," said Christine. "Not with that ankle. And you've nowhere to go."

"If I could get to London," Dave said, "I might be able to get work. Or if I could get to Germany, Vikki would help me."

"But you haven't got any money," Christine said.

"But I'm not going to get any money sitting here, am I?" he said.

"But you've got to get your foot better first," said Lucy. "You can't go to Germany on that foot."

"I thought my ankle would be better long before this," he said. "I thought it might only be twisted. But I suppose there must be something serious wrong with it. Maybe it's broke. Perhaps it really would be best to give myself up."

"But you can't give up now," I said.

Now I wonder how much we forced him to go on. How much he felt he had to do it for us. But I didn't think of that then.

"We've got to think of something," Christine said.

"But you'd better get out of here," Lucy said. "Just in case."

So we sat there and tried to think of something.

"Your foot is getting better," said Christine. "Isn't it?"

"Well it's not as bad as it was," he said.

"Is it still painful?" asked Lucy.

"Well, yeah. It's still pretty painful."

"Perhaps it just needs a few more days," Christine said.

"Yeah. Maybe."

"If only you could rest it for another couple of days," she said.

"But he can't stay here," said Lucy.

"Then we'll have to think of somewhere he can go to rest it," Christine said.

We were quiet for a bit because nobody could think of anything. Then suddenly I had an idea. The very place.

"I know," I said. "The island. The island in the river."

"What island?" said Dave.

"Oh yeah," said Terry. "Treasure Island."

"But how would he get there?" said Christine. "He can't walk that far."

"We can go on the bus," I said.

"Don't be stupid," she said. "We won't have enough money."

"Well, there must be some way," I said.

Terry said, "Let's go on a boat down the river."

"We haven't got a boat," said Christine.

"Well let's pinch one," said Lucy.

"No," said Dave. "Now listen. You mustn't pinch anything. I don't want any of you getting in trouble."

"We don't care," said Lucy.

"Well, I care," said Dave. "That would make me wish I'd never escaped in the first place. And if you don't care about it for yourself, think of me. Because when I'm caught, if they can say I've led you into trouble, I'll get a longer sentence than ever."

"Well, we'll make a boat then," said Lucy.

"How can we make a boat?" asked Christine.

"We could make a raft," I said.

"Now wait a minute," said Dave. "What is all this? What island?"

"There's this great island in the river," Terry said.

"Our dad took us there on the holidays," I said. "It was great. You could build a great hide-out there."

"How far is it?" he said.

"Oh, it's not far," I said. "It's only just

down the river." It hadn't seemed very far in our car.

"And how would I get to the river?" he said.

"If we make a raft," I said, "we could go down the canal to the aqueduct and then carry it down the steps to the river."

"It's only about half a mile to the aqueduct," Terry said.

"Go on, Dave. Let's do it," I said.

Dave looked at me all serious for a moment, and then he smiled. "Why not?" he said. "Why not? If I get caught, I get caught."

"Tomorrow's Saturday," Christine said. "We'll get a load of food in the morning."

"And how will I recognize your island when I get to it?" Dave said.

"We'll show you," said Terry.

"We're all coming," said Lucy.

"But how will you get back?" he said.

We couldn't think of the answer to that problem for a moment. Then Christine said, "It's all right. We'll go on the bus. I'll tell the conductor I've lost my purse with all our money in, and give him a false name and address."

Dave laughed. "In the army, they used to give us initiative tests. You lot would do all right in them. They'd make you all officers straightaway. Anyway, look at the time. You'd better get off home to supper."

"We'll come back after and build the raft," I said.

"What'll we need for the raft?" said Christine.

"Well, we've got plenty of wood here," said Dave. "We can use floorboards for the frame, and a door for the deck. We've got our bit of rope, but we'll need more of that, if you can get any. And we'll need a hammer and nails. If you can't get a hammer, bring a heavy stone I can hold in my hand to hit the nails with. Like a Stone Age man with a primitive tool. And if you can't get any nails, we'll use nails out of these floorboards when we take them up. The only difficult thing will be finding something for buoyancy."

"What's that?" I said.

"To make us float."

"Wood floats," I said.

"But with us lot on, it wouldn't float very well," he said. "And we wouldn't get along very fast. We need some empty oil drums, or something like that."

"I know where there's some of them," said Terry. "Right near where we live. On the dump by the pub."

"Well bring them tonight," Dave said. "After supper."

I don't think he believed it was really going to happen. But *we* did.

FIVE

After supper I nipped down into our cellar. I found a box of nails and a hammer and another piece of rope. Then Chris and me went to call for Lucy, and then Terry. We went down behind the pub where the old coalman's stables used to be. The stables had been pulled down, and everybody chucked their rubbish there. We found four oil drums. Big ones. We each took one and rolled it up the hill to the canal wall. The drums were really heavy. We had to all roll one at a time up the wall, and shove it over the top, so that it crashed and boinged on the towpath. Then we rolled them along to the house.

Dave was really surprised when he saw what we'd got. We didn't make the raft that evening, because we wouldn't of been able to get it out the window. But we worked out how to make it and got everything ready, so we could just put it together the next morning.

I couldn't get to sleep that night for excitement. It poured with rain again. I could hear it pounding against my window as I lay in bed. I hadn't really thought before about what it was like for Dave in his cold room with the window that didn't have any glass in it. And now I didn't think about how much worse it would be when he was living out on the island, without even an old house to stay in. I just thought about what an adventure it would be to build the raft and go down the river.

Saturday morning was drizzly. Dad slept late, luckily, or he might of asked us what was up. Mum couldn't understand what was the matter with Chris and me, rushing out so early. We called for the others. Terry's mum went off the deep because he hadn't had his breakfast. But he came anyway. Lucy was just coming out to call for us when we got to her back-yard gate.

We'd all got bags with food stuffed up inside our coats. We went around to a shop a few streets away. We all gave our money to Christine. She went in and bought more food and some matches. She tried to buy Dave some cigarettes as well but the woman wouldn't sell her any because she saw us waiting outside and thought we wanted to smoke them ourselves. So Chris got another jelly roll instead.

We went a roundabout way. When we whistled up to Dave, he slung his rucksack down. Then he slung down the floorboards and the door and rope and everything. He went down to the cellar and came out that way. He was limping bad. He only had one shoe on because his ankle was still too swollen to get the other on. He'd still got Christine's radio as well, which he'd forgot to give her the night before. She said he could keep it for his camp on the island. We humped all the stuff over the wall onto the towpath.

Christine said, "It *would* rain."

"Just as well really," Dave said. "There's less likelihood of anyone else coming along in the rain."

He knocked together an oblong frame for the raft with the floorboards. He nailed a door across for the deck. Then we held up the frame for him, while he tied two of the oil drums in at one end and hacked off the spare piece of rope with his knife. He joined that piece to the other bit I'd found in our cellar, and tied the other two drums in at the other end. He said, "There's not enough rope, really. I hope that's going to do."

We piled all our stuff onto the raft, and then we had to drag it into the canal. It was really heavy. We had to walk into the water up to our waists to get it in. But it floated terrific. We all got on board and it was great. The deck was just under the water. We sat on the oil drums and we had pieces of floorboards to paddle with. Four of us could paddle at once. Me and Terry were on one side. When he paddled, he splashed water all over me, so I splashed him. Christine told us to keep quiet, but Dave said it didn't matter.

Then Spotty Sally came along the tow-path. She saw us and started running up and down, barking and wagging her tail. She plunged into the canal and swam over to us and climbed up on board the raft. Then she stood up all soaking, and shook herself, and sprayed everybody with cold water. We kept telling her to go back, but she wouldn't. We pushed her in, but she just climbed back onto the raft and sprayed everybody again. So we let her stay.

We were all laughing at first, and really pleased with ourselves, but after we'd been paddling for a bit we realized we weren't getting along very fast.

"This'll take hours to get to the aqueduct," Christine said.

"Yeah," said Dave. "This is no good. We'll have to get Spotty Sally to pull us along like a barge horse."

"We could pull you along," said Terry.

"We haven't got any rope," I said.

Dave said, "What about a floorboard? If I held one end on the raft, could you pull the other end?"

So Terry and me and Spotty Sally got off

the raft and ran back to the house. We went around to the front and got into the cellar and went upstairs. Terry started to pry up a floorboard, but then I had an idea.

"Hey, Terry, what about this?" The wire for the electric light was hanging down from the ceiling.

"Wow, yeah!" he said. We got hold of it and pulled and pulled as hard as we could. Spotty Sally got the end of the wire in her mouth and started pulling as well. Then suddenly the wire came away and all this plaster fell down from the ceiling, all over us. It didn't hurt really, but we fell down on the floor. We got covered with plaster dust, and it all went in our eyes and nose and mouth. It was horrible. Still, we had a great long piece of wire.

We ran back to the raft.

"What's the matter with you lot?" said Dave. "You look like ghosts."

"The ceiling fell on us," I said. "But look what we got."

When we got to the aqueduct, we had to get the raft down the steps to the riverbank. The drums were easy. We just rolled them down. They didn't half make a racket. Dave didn't seem to mind about the noise. It was almost as if he half wanted to get caught. Then all four of us got one end of the raft and dragged it down. Dave couldn't help because he needed his hands to hold on to the handrail. He just carried his rucksack, and the ropes, and the food and things, which was quite a lot, actually.

But you should of seen the river. It was much wider and deeper than usual because of all the rain. It was all brown and flowing ever so fast.

Dave stood watching the river for a bit, looking worried. Then he got to work and rebuilt the raft. Then when it was ready, he said, "I'm sorry kids, but you can't come."

"What do you mean?" asked Christine.

"Sorry," he said. "But it's just out of the question."

"But it was my idea," I said. "I'm going to come."

"None of you are going to come."

"You can't do that," said Lucy. "That's betraying us."

"It's not, Luce. It's not that."

"It is! It is!" she yelled.

"No," he said. "Look at the river. It's too dangerous."

"No it's not," said Terry. "It's a great raft. It floats great. We've tried it out already."

"But none of you've got life jackets. You should never ever go on the water without life jackets."

"You haven't got a life jacket," said Christine.

"But I can swim."

"Well, we can swim," said Lucy.

"All of you?"

"Yes," said Christine. "I've got my bronze, and my lifesaver's."

"But even so . . ."

"We can all swim," I said. "We go at school. I can do a length. And my dad takes us."

"But swimming in a pool isn't the same as being in a fast river. Especially when it's so cold."

"We often swim in this river," said Christine. "We come here all the time."

"Anyway," I said, "I'm coming. You

can't leave us behind. We're blood brothers."

"I know," he said. "But that's just it. I love you. I love you more than I've ever loved anybody in my life. Supposing something happened to you?"

"Well you can't leave us behind," said Christine.

"All right then. I'll give myself up."

I ran at him and started punching him as hard as I could. "You can't do that," I said. "We've looked after you all this time so you could get away."

I really hurt him, so he got hold of my arms to stop me from hitting him anymore. "I'd rather go to prison than risk your lives," he said.

"Well you can't go to prison," Christine said. "You've got to get away."

"And I'm coming with you," I said.

"So am I," said Terry.

"We're all coming," said Lucy.

"We're all blood brothers and sisters," said Christine, "so we've got to stay together."

"Oh God!" said Dave.

"Come on," said Christine. "Let's launch our boat."

Dave was nearly crying. He shook his head. "Oh Christ!" he said. "What a bunch you are."

We started to drag the raft into the water. Dave stood there watching for a minute. Then he said, "O.K. But listen. I'm the captain of this boat. Right? Because I'm the oldest. So you must do exactly what I say. Is that agreed?"

We all cheered him, and he came to help us.

"We ought to have a name," I said. "We ought to have a name for our boat."

"O.K.," said Dave. "What shall we call it?"

"Let's call it the *Jolly Roger*," said Terry.

"What about the *River Racer*?" said Lucy.

I thought and thought but I couldn't think of anything good.

"I know," said Christine. "This raft is going to help Dave escape, so let's call it *Freedom*."

"Yeah," I said. "That's a great name."

"O.K.," said Dave. "I name this raft *Freedom*, and good luck to all who ride on it."

We dragged *Freedom* into the river. Luckily it was quite slow at the side. We got afloat and all clambered on board. We kept pushing Spotty Sally off because we didn't want her to come down the river, but she just swam after us and came on board again so we had to let her stay. Dave sat in the middle and gave orders. Spotty kept coming around and licking everybody in the face. Dave told which ones to paddle so that we always kept in the fast part of the current. He'd made the deck higher out of the water, but on the river there were all sorts of swirls and little waves, and with the splashing from the paddles, we got soaked through. The drizzle kept on. It was stinging my face like lots and lots of tiny needles. It was freezing, but no one complained of being cold because we were all proud of being on board *Freedom*.

Dave gave everybody food out of the pack that we had given him. At first we wouldn't take it because that was all he would have to live on, but it must of been after lunchtime and we were starving, so in the end we all took some.

We didn't see anybody. We just passed between trees, all wet and leafy, and then fields with cows standing about eating. They were out in the rain all the time, and they never made a fuss. They didn't seem to mind at all, but I wished the rain would stop so I could get a bit warmer.

The river kept bending about. We had to keep crossing from side to side to stay with the fast current. If we got left on the wrong side we slowed down till we nearly stopped. When it was my side that had to paddle it was really hard work.

Suddenly we came around a bend and we were going toward where all these trees were leaning out right low over the water.

"Lucy and Chris, paddle! Paddle like mad! Andy and Terry, paddle backward! Backward! Faster! Come on, come on!" Dave cried. But the river just carried us straight on toward the trees.

"Lay flat! Right down! Flat!" And I felt Dave's hand grab my arm, and Terry lying across my legs, and my head was crushed up against Dave's body. I could feel the cold of the water covering the deck and smell the strong smell of Dave's wet clothes. And then there was the swooshing and scraping of the leaves and branches over the front of the raft, and then over us. We were covered and brushed and dusted and scratched and hit. I yelled and closed my eyes. I could hear Dave's voice saying, "It's all right, kids. Hang on to the raft and hang on to each other." And then the swooshing passed over the back of the raft and the noise stopped. I opened my eyes and we all sat up.

"Are we all here?" said Dave. "Anybody get swept overboard?"

"I'm all scratched," said Christine. We all were.

"Where's Spotty?" yelled Lucy.

Spotty Sally wasn't on the raft. We looked back. All we could see was the heavy wet green curtain of the trees, brushing the frothing bubbling brown water that surged out from under it. But no Spotty Sally.

"Spotty!"

"Sally!"

"Sal!"

"Paddle backward," said Dave. "Everybody. Paddle backward as hard as you can to slow us down."

We paddled frantically and called and called, and then we saw the black face bob up this side of the trees. We paddled harder than ever and called louder.

"Spotty! Come on! Swim! Come on girl! Come on Sal!" She swam like mad and the river helped her shoot down toward us. We paddled backward until she caught us. We dragged her on board and everyone cuddled her and stroked her and kissed her, even though she was soaking wet and cold, and nobody minded when she kept shaking herself all over us, or licking us in the eye or mouth.

It was all right for a bit after that. We passed the place where we usually went swimming. There were no people on the little sandy beach, but some cows had come down where we played, and they were standing with their feet in the water drinking from the river. They stopped drinking as we passed and looked at us. "They must think we're barmy," said Dave.

We sailed on quite a way further. I was just about frozen to death. The water was stinging my scratches. I was glad when I had to paddle because it helped me get a bit warmer. Then the bits of floorboard started to hurt my hands so much, I didn't want to paddle anymore. I was really miserable and felt like crying. But nobody else cried or made a fuss, so I didn't either.

We came around a bend and there was a long straight bit of river. The noise of the river seemed to be getting louder as we went along. And we seemed to be getting faster. I looked down ahead and Dave was looking too. He got up onto his knees, and then stood up, so he could see better. I looked at his face. He was really worried. The noise was getting louder and we were gaining speed. We started going really fast then. Speed fast. Up ahead the water wasn't smooth, but all broken up. All rough and bouncy. We started going faster than ever and bumping up and down more.

"Andy and Terry! Paddle! Paddle, boys, as hard as you can! Chris, Luce, paddle backward! Quick! Quick!"

"What's the matter, Dave? Is it a water-fall?" I said.

"No. No. It's rapids. Paddle now. Let's get over to the side."

But we just went faster. We kept going faster, and the noise was like a roar. I was scared. I started to cry a little bit, but I tried not to let it show. Anyhow, I had rain all over my face, so no one could tell. I paddled as hard as I could even though my hands were hurting, but the raft just went plunging, like a bucking bronco, straight on.

"Give me the paddle!" Dave shouted. He pushed me into the middle of the raft. He started to paddle as hard as he could, but it didn't make any difference.

"Hang on to the raft!" he shouted. "Just hang on!" I grabbed hold of the edge of the deck, but as we bounced the oil drum smashed against my fingers. I yelled and let go. I was slung about the deck, sliding all over the place and bumping into people. Christine screamed out, "I've lost my pad-dle!"

"Don't worry. Don't worry. It doesn't

matter. Just hang on!" Dave had stopped paddling too. We all just hung on and some of us were screaming. And then *crash* and then *crash* again, and then all the time, *bang, bang, bang*, and we all started yelling.

"It's all right," yelled Dave. "It's all right. Really. We're just banging on the rocks on the bottom of the river. That just means it's shallow. That means we're safe."

But he didn't convince anybody. The banging went on. And we all went on crying. And then Christine did a terrible loud scream. "Dave!" she yelled. Dave had jumped off the side of the raft and was in the water. He was hanging on to the raft and being dragged along.

"I'm making it lighter," he yelled, "so it doesn't bang so much." But it went faster still and he had to drag himself back on board. Then Terry screamed out and kept on screaming. No one knew what was the matter. "It's all right," Dave kept saying. "It's all right." But Terry just pointed and kept on. Then we saw what he was yelling about. One of our oil drums was floating off down the river in front of us, like a wheel

that's fallen off your car when you're going at top speed, and it was going even faster than we were. It had been the one that Terry had been sitting on. He just felt it bounce away, and he gripped onto the raft, but he thought it was all breaking up. The water poured and splashed all over us, and the river roared, and the raft was tipped down at one corner now.

Bang, bang, bang, CRASH! We screamed, we didn't know what was happening. The icy water was pouring over us, but we were still hanging on to the raft, which was tipped up more than ever. But the banging had stopped. And we were still. It took a little while to realize it. What had happened was that we'd struck against a huge rock, and wedged. Terry and Lucy and Dave were down in the water with just their heads sticking out like seals. But Christine and me were just up to our waists. Spotty Sally kept scrabbling up and sliding down again over and over.

"Where's the stuff?" yelled Lucy. I could see Dave's rucksack floating away at top speed, and some of the food bags, but not the hammer and radio and that.

"Never mind about that." said Dave. "Just as long as we're all safe." Well, I didn't feel very safe stuck there in the middle of this river, with icy water bursting all over me at about a hundred miles an hour, but I didn't say anything. Dave was talking loud in a very calm voice.

"Now listen," he said. "Please, please, let's have no more screaming and crying. It won't help anything. Everybody's safe. Nobody's hurt. Everything's going to be all right. We're in a difficult position, and we've got to think quietly and calmly about what the best thing is to do. Now please. It doesn't help to scream at a time like this. Now keep calm and everything will be all right."

Dave looked around at the river for a bit. Then at the bank. "Right," he said. "We're quite close to this side. I'll try it out first to see if it's all right. Then I'll come back and get you. Now just hang on to the raft."

He got hold of a rock sticking out of the water with one hand, and lowered himself into the river. As he took his weight off the raft, it began to lift up in the water, and we all screamed again. "It's all right," said Dave. "Sit tight." Then, sitting on the edge of the raft, he dipped into the water like a duck feeding, and came up with rocks off the river bed that he could hardly lift. He heaped rocks onto the raft and then he carefully got off again. This time the raft stayed where it was. The water was rushing by at terrific speed making a really loud roaring noise like a giant machine. There were rocks sticking up everywhere, like river monsters poking their heads out of the water to watch us. The rushing water divided around them and swelled up into waves like you get in a rough sea.

Dave let go of the raft and stepped into the current, and then he just got swept away. He just disappeared. Then we saw him bobbing up and down, bouncing over rocks, and being thrown in and out of the angry rushing river, as it carried him along like an old piece of broken wood. He struggled and struggled, but it didn't make any difference. The river was in charge. And the monsters just stood and watched. Christine shouted out, "Daaaaave!" in a long-drawn-out scream that made my hair stand on end. By the time she got to the end of it, Dave was a hundred yards downstream and we could hardly see him. Just a glimpse of his green anorak. But then we saw him getting closer to the bank.

He climbed ever so slowly up the bank, like in a slow-motion film, as if he was very heavy and it was painful for him to move. Then he knelt up and waved to us. We all waved back, relieved that he wasn't drowned, partly for him and partly for us. After a moment he got up and began to hobble along the bank toward us as fast as he could. He fell down about four or five times. Lucy yelled out, "Good old Dave," and we all waved. We just had to sit there in the water till he got up level with us. He shouted to us but we could hardly hear him above the roar of the water. I think he was saying, "Just hang on!" and something else.

Then he hobbled further upstream past us. I thought for a moment he was going to go away and leave us. I got a pain as though strong icy fingers had got hold of whatever

I've got inside my stomach, and had twisted them up. I shouted out to him but he couldn't hear. Then he made his way down the bank to the edge of the water by sliding on his backside. He stood up, and suddenly threw himself out into the river again. He swam like mad, as though he was trying to swim across the river, but he was being swept down the river sideways. He was trying to get far enough out to reach us before the river brought him level with us. We all yelled, "Come on, Dave! Come on, Dave!" But he was coming down too fast. As he came level he gave up swimming and reached out his hands, and I saw his eyes scared and his mouth open and the river water gushing into his face. I stretched out to him but I couldn't reach him and he was past. But then he jolted up against a rock, and he threw his arms around it. The river was trying to carry his legs away and he struggled against the water. It looked as though he was wrestling with this big river monster. Gradually he managed to haul himself to his feet and drag himself onto the raft. We all hugged each other all at once.

Even Spotty Sally tried to join in the hugging. But we soon realized that we were right back as we were when we first crashed.

"I've got a new respect for water," Dave said. "I never believed it could be so strong."

"What are we going to do?" said Lucy.

"We'll try the other way," said Dave. "I should think more before acting. I went to that bank because it's much nearer. But that way, although it's further, looks shallower, and not so fast."

"Oh please don't leave us again," said Christine.

"No. O.K., I'll tell you what we'll do. We'll all go together," he said. "We'll rope up and link hands and walk slowly over to that bank. It's not so deep this side, so if you fall down don't worry about it because you won't drown. As long as we keep linked up you won't get carried away. But don't let go of the person you're holding, whatever you do. Keep hold, whether you fall down or whatever. The other person's life might depend on it. Or your own might. So keep hold. As long as we keep hold, nothing can happen. If somebody falls down, everybody else just stand still till they find their feet again. O.K.?"

"What about Spotty?" I asked.

"She'll be all right," said Dave. "She'll look after herself."

Dave untied the rope off the end of the raft, and the raft lurched, and another oil drum leapt free and raced bouncing away from us down the river. Dave slid into the water on the other side of the raft. The water was about waist deep on him, but where it hit against him it sort of climbed up his body, and he had to cling to the raft to stop being swept away. He climbed back onto the raft. "It's too strong," he said. "We'll have to rope up first." He looped the rope over himself. Then he wound one end around me and Terry, and the other end around Lucy and Christine. "We'll hold hands," he said, "and you two on the ends, with your spare hands, keep hold of the ends of the rope, and keep it pulled tight."

Holding on to the raft, he lowered himself into the river again. "Come on, Luce," he said. "Hold on to me. Just cling to me till everybody's in, and then we can link up." Lucy got into the water, and I slid in next to Dave on the other side.

"Hang on," he said crossly. "One at a time."

The river pressed me hard against Dave. Then Terry came next to me and he got rammed up against me. Then the raft suddenly lifted with Christine and Spotty Sally still on it. Christine screamed and Dave grabbed her coat and yelled, "Jump! Jump!"

Christine jumped into the river and fell right down under the water. Dave fell as well, and when he fell the rest of us fell down too and the freezing water gushed over my head and filled my eyes and mouth and nose, and we were all pushed along and smashed up against the big rock the raft had been jammed against. I was pressed against the rock with the water crashing against my chest so it felt like my rib cage would collapse. I could hardly breathe. I swallowed lots of water and choked.

"Where's Spotty?" someone yelled. I could see the raft bouncing away at top speed down the river, but Spotty Sally wasn't on it. Then Dave said, "I can see her."

"Where?"

"Look, look. There she is."

"Where?"

"She's all right. She's swimming."

And there she was. Swimming toward the bank. She was being carried sideways down the river, but she was still managing to make headway across as well.

"Right, come on. Link up," Dave said. "Don't hold hands. Grip each other's wrists. Like this."

We set off from the stone out into the river. Terry was the first to go down because he was the one to have the full force of the river on him. Dave stumbled at nearly every step because he could hardly walk on his ankle. All of us fell at times. Once we all fell down at the same time. When you fell, the water would drag you along a bit, but there was always somebody holding both your arms, and the rope was around your stomach, so no one got swept away. Spotty came bounding up the bank and barked to us. She kept plunging into the water to meet us, but then she'd get washed over and she'd go back and bark to us again. As we got closer to the bank the water was less deep and less strong, but the rocks were rounded and green and slippery so we still kept falling. But we got to the bank at last. And Spotty Sally jumped all over us.

We rested for a while, but we were all shaking with cold, so we got up and stomped around on our sore feet. Teeth chattering. We were all soaked right through, and our shoes squelched with every step. Dave said we ought to take off most of our clothes and wring them out or we'd never dry. We were all bruised. But Dave was the worst. We squeezed our things out and got dressed again as quick as possible. The drizzle had stopped, but the sky was still all gray. It must have been about suppertime.

We set off walking along the bank. Around the next turn we could see the bridge that led to the little town where Dad and I went to get the fuse. So it wasn't all that far to the island. We were going across bumpy fields so we couldn't get on very fast. We took it in turns to help Dave. He sort of hopped along between two of us, with his hands on our shoulders.

It wasn't all that far, but it took a terrible long time. I suppose it was about a mile. We had to cross a road. Then we went along by the river again. Around a bend. Then we came to the steps where we'd played when Mum and Dad were burying the treasure. You can't get any further along by the river there because the bank starts to go straight up, like a cliff. So we went up the giant steps. Dave went up on all fours, like a dog. But he got up really quick. Then we went down the path through the trees. Over the broken bridge. There was a stream, almost a waterfall pouring under it this time. And down to the island.

Our tree-trunk bridge was still there, although the water was about three inches under it, instead of three feet. Christine and me went across with Dave, holding his hands. It was getting evening by then. Dave said we had to go back home. We wanted to

help him make a den, but he wouldn't let us. He said our parents would have the police out looking for us if we weren't home before dark.

"We'll come tomorrow," I said.

"How will you manage that?" he said.

"I don't know."

"Well whatever you do," he said, "don't come on a raft."

"Not bloody likely," I said.

So we left him there. We walked back up the path. He stood waving to us. I felt really sorry for him. I felt sorry for myself too, but at least I could go back to my warm dry home. We left him there all wet and cold and alone, with night coming on and nowhere to sleep and no food. For us the game was over. But it wasn't a game for him.

We walked to the town to get a bus, and luckily there was a bus standing there in the main square. The driver and conductor weren't on it, but some people were sitting there. We went right up the back and sat on the long seat. Spotty Sally kept trying to sit on our laps, but she was all wet and we kept pushing her off. I couldn't stop my teeth chattering, but it was nice and warm on the bus. We all sat up close together. We were worrying about whether the conductor would put us off when he found we didn't have any money.

After a bit the driver and conductor got on. The driver started off and the conductor stayed at the front talking to him for a while. Then he came around collecting the fares. We were last. When he came to the back he looked at us and his bushy eyebrows went up and down a few times. Then he said, "What have you lot been up to then?"

"Please, sir," said Christine, "we all fell in the river, and I've lost my purse with all our money in."

"You fell in the river, did you? My goodness, you'll all be catching your death of cold. Whatever's your mother going to say when you get home?"

"I don't know," said Christine.

"And is this your dog?"

"Yes."

"Well, he's supposed to have a collar and lead on to come on the bus, you know."

"Oh," said Christine.

Then Lucy said, "We lost them in the river and all."

"Did you now?" said the conductor. And his eyebrows shot up and down a few more times, faster than ever. "And you've lost all your money, eh? Dear oh dear. You are in a pickle. Well never mind about that. But you'd just better take more care in future." He smiled at us and shook his head. Then he went back down the bus closing the open windows.

The next thing to worry about was what our parents were going to say that night. And then, how we were going to get back to Dave with some food the next day.

SIX

When the bus pulled in at the bus station, the first thing we saw was my dad's car. Dad was standing beside it, talking to a man in a bus uniform. He looked up and saw us. I had a funny feeling. I wanted to shrink down out of sight so he wouldn't see me, and at the same time I wanted him to come and lift me off the bus and take me home.

We got off the bus and Dad came over to us. He looked quickly at each of us, as though to satisfy himself we were all complete.

"Are you all right?" he said. "No one hurt? All right. Jump in the car." He didn't say anything else, but he was pretty angry.

You could tell. Not shouting-out angry. But sort of quiet, controlled angry. He got into the driver's seat and we set off home. It's only a couple of minutes to our house.

Dad said, "Well you lot have a load of explaining to do. But first you can all get into dry clothes, and get some grub inside you. Then I want to hear the story. And it better be a good one." He didn't say anything else.

He drove to our house and told us all to get inside. We didn't even have a chance to say good-by to Spotty Sally. Terry and Lucy were pleased because they were scared of going to their own homes. Dad went in first and called out, "I've got four drowned rats here, Love. Have we got any water for the bath?"

"Oh, you've found them," Mum said. "Where are they?" She came running out of the kitchen. "Are you all right, Loves?"

"Yes, Mum," said Christine. Mum kissed Christine and me.

"Well what have you been up to?" she said. "I've been worried out of my wits."

Dad said, "Let them get into some dry clothes first, and have a nosh. They can tell us all about it then."

"Well get up to the bathroom, all of you," Mum said. "There's plenty of hot water. Andy, you and Terry go in first. And lend Terry some clothes. And then you girls."

Then Dad came toward us. His face looked really ugly and angry. He jabbed one finger at us. "And I want you in and out of that bath and dressed by the time I get back. Understand? In and out in two minutes. And dressed. And I don't want no mucking about. I'm going to tell Lucy's and Terry's parents they're here and they're safe, and that we'll give them their supper, and that the police can come and see you all here. They won't want the police going around to their houses. And by the time I get back you'd better all be dressed and sitting at that table."

The police! We looked at each other but no one said anything. Dad went on out, thank goodness, and Terry and me nipped upstairs and had a quick bath. It was the quickest bath I've ever had in my life, I can tell you. My dad's all right most of the time. But when he's in one of them moods, he's like a dangerous lunatic. You never know what he's going to do. Best thing is to do whatever he says. Humor him.

Anyway he was gone quite a long time, luckily. When he came back we were all having eggs and sausages and chips. Then, when we finished that, we all had to go and sit on the settee. We just left the plates on the table. Mum and Dad came and sat in front of us. Mum in the armchair and Dad brought a chair over from the table. It was peculiar. It was all sort of formal, like a court.

Dad said, "The police were around here this afternoon. They were at Terry's house first. Then they came here. And then they went to Lucy's. I told the police I'd let them know as soon as you came home. Now, I haven't let them know. Yet. I don't know what you've been up to, and I don't know the rights and wrongs of it. But I want to know. I want to know the whole story. And while you're about it you can tell me where my hammer's gone."

"Yes. And you can explain what you've been doing with all the food you've been taking out of the cupboard as well," Mum said. "I don't know if you thought I haven't noticed, because I have. I'm not so green as I'm cabbage-looking."

"Well?" said Dad. "Let's have it."

None of us said a word. There was a long silence. I could hear our clock ticking. And voices from next door's television. Bill Smithson went up the road on his motor-bike. And some dogs barked. I wondered if one of them was Spotty Sally. Mum and Dad just sat looking at us without saying a word.

I said, "We can't tell you, Dad. We promised."

Dad looked at me. He nodded his head slowly. "*I* might think that was a good reason, Son, but the police won't." His voice was much softer. "All you kids know that whatever you've done, Mum and me will stand by you. We don't want you to get into trouble, any of you."

"Of course we don't," said Mum. "You can tell us."

"If we know the whole story, we'll be able to advise you."

"But Dad," I said. "We promised. We're blood brothers."

"Who are?" Dad said.

I started crying. I couldn't help it. It seemed like not to tell was betraying my dad, but telling would be betraying Dave. I looked at the others. "Let's tell them," I said.

They were all nearly crying as well, but no one answered.

"Would you promise to keep a secret, Dad, if we told you?" I asked.

"No, Andy. I don't think I could promise that. But you know I'd do my best for you, don't you."

"But it's not us, Dad. It's for someone else. He needs help, and we promised to help him."

"Well if there's someone needs help," Mum said, "and we can help him, then we will."

I looked at the others again. "Let's tell," I said.

So we told them the whole story. Everything. All about Dave, and him deserting from the army, and escaping from the police. And about how we'd taken him food to the house. And about the raft, and everything. They just listened. Right to the end. Then a funny thing happened. Dad started to cry. He didn't make a noise. He just looked at us, and there were tears formed in his eyes.

"You're good kids," he said. "I wish I'd had some friends like you when I was younger."

Christine went and sat on Mum's lap, and I went to Dad, and he put his arms around me.

"You might of all been drowned," Mum said.

Dad said, "Well, I'll have to go and phone to the police in a moment. I don't know what you're going to tell them."

"I'm not going to tell them anything," I said.

"Neither am I," said Christine.

"Well, they know what he looks like already," Dad said. "And what he was wearing. So it can't hurt to tell them that. And seeing as he's gone from the old house now, it can't hurt to tell them he was there. And they'll also want to know where you were all day today, so you'd better think about that. Anyway I'd better go down and phone them now."

Well it was like Dad was giving us some advice. So that's what we did. When the policemen came, we told them where Dave had been, and how we took him food. But we said he'd gone now. The policemen were all right. They didn't try to bully us or anything. They were just dead friendly. Too friendly really. As though they were just pretending to be ever so friendly when they didn't like us at all really. They gave us a long boring lecture about how it was good to uphold the law and help the police in a difficult job to apprehend villains and all stuff like that. Of course they didn't know Dave wasn't a villain. They'd never met him. And if they did catch him, they wouldn't get to know him and find out how kind he was. They just wanted to "bring him to justice." What they meant was, they wanted to punish him for not wanting to kill people in Ireland. Then they asked us lots of questions. Like where had he gone and that.

Christine said, "We don't know where he went. He didn't say."

The heavy policeman with the moustache smiled and smiled. "But you must have some idea where he was going. From something he said. You must have picked up some clues—sharp kids like you. What about you, chuck?" he said to Lucy. "He must have said something about it. Didn't he? Perhaps not to the others. Just to you?"

"Yes, he did," said Lucy. I looked at her to warn her, but she didn't look at me. She just smiled at the policeman. And his smile changed so that he really did look pleased for a moment. "He said he was going to catch a bus," Lucy said, and smiled sweetly. The skin on the policeman's face went tight, and made it hard for him to keep smiling.

"Where to?" the policeman asked.

"I don't know," said Lucy, smiling, "he didn't say."

They even said that we might get a reward if we helped them. And they said we might find ourselves in real trouble if we kept back any information. But it didn't make any difference. Then they wanted to know where we'd been, so we told them how we'd made the raft and been paddling it along the canal. And then I had a good idea. I said some men came along on a cabin cruiser and Terry called out, "Give us a ride, Mister," and this fellow said, "All right." I told them about the time when we really did go up the canal on a boat. I said that we all had a go at steering and that they took us miles and miles. Then we had to walk back and it took us ages. The tall policeman tried to catch me out, and he asked me what the cabin cruiser had been like, and what the men were like, but I told him everything I could remember about the real boat, and the real men, and about what they told us about the big barges in Germany and everything. So then he seemed satisfied.

Mum and Dad were there. They didn't say anything. Except when the policemen were going, Dad said, "They're all very good kids. I'm proud of them."

As soon as the policemen left, Dad said me and Christine had to go to bed.

"But what are we going to do about Dave, Dad?" Christine said.

"I don't know," he said. "Mum and me'll have a talk about it. We'll see in the morning."

Dad took Lucy and Terry home. He said he'd talk to their parents so they wouldn't get in too much trouble. And he said he'd ask if they could come out with us the next day.

Mum came into our bedroom. She kissed me good night. Then she stayed sitting on the side of my bed. "I hope you don't tell lies to me," she said.

"No, Mum," I said. "I don't need to."

Next morning Mum and Dad made up two big packs of picnic. We called for the others and we all went out in the car. Of course we went straight to the island. We left the stuff in the car and Mum and Dad began walking slowly down to the island. We ran on ahead.

We whistled before we went onto the island, and we heard Dave whistle back. We couldn't find him at first. He'd made himself a shelter out of wood and leaves and he was really well camouflaged. We found him at last. He was lying inside his shelter on the ground. He looked really ill. His ankle was swollen up again, worse than ever.

"You all all right?" he said.

"Yeah," I said.

"Well I'm certainly glad to see you."

"Our mum and dad's coming," Christine said. Dave looked scared so she said, "But they're O.K."

"They're friends," I said.

Terry said, "The police came. But it was all right."

"We didn't tell them nothing," I said.

"I told them you'd gone away on a bus," said Lucy.

Then Mum and Dad came. We all had to get out of the way. Dave dragged himself out of the little shelter and sat on the ground. Dad didn't look all that pleased, but he shook hands with Dave, and so did Mum.

"I hear you're in a bit of trouble," Dad said.

"Yeah," said Dave.

"You might of killed them all," Mum said.

Dave said, "I'm sorry."

Dad said, "Well, what are you going to do?"

Dave said, "I don't know. I can't really do much. I suppose I've had it."

Dad sat down on the ground too. "I've been in trouble myself," he said. "The thing is, once you get on the skids, you just get in deeper and deeper." He looked at Dave and Dave looked at him and nodded. It was funny. When we'd been just with Dave, he always seemed like a grown-up. But now he was talking to my dad, he seemed like a little boy—like me or Terry.

"I don't know what you're going to do," Dad said. "I don't want to encourage you to keep on running, but if you are going to, we'll give you a hand."

"We've got food in the car," Mum said.

"We'll give you a hand either way," Dad said.

"I think the first thing, Love, is, he needs something to eat and a hot drink," Mum said.

"Well I don't like to give up now," Dave said. He looked over at us. "Not after all this. I feel I'd be letting them down."

I think Dad was pleased really. He said, "Well, we've brought a change of clothes, and food, and a few pounds to help you on your way. After that you're on your own. We can take you to the nearest railway station. Or we can take you back home and call the police."

"I'll go to the station," Dave said. "I'll try and get to London. I'll be able to see a doctor there."

"In the meantime," Mum said, "let's get you up to the car, and see what we can do for you for the time being."

Dad gave Dave a piggyback up the hill. And that took some doing. Me and Terry tried giving each other piggybacks too, but it was hard work. We got to the car and Dave changed into some of Dad's baggy old clothes. He put his own things in a carrier to take with him. Dave only had one shoe because none of Dad's would fit. Mum and Dad tore up some old rag they'd got in the car, and bound Dave's ankle up with it, and used a piece of wood for a splint. They said they didn't know if it would do any good, but they didn't know what else to do. Then we had our picnic and shared it with Dave. The other bag of food was for him to take with him.

Then we drove on to the next town where there was a station. There wasn't a London train for a couple of hours, so we just sat in the car and talked. Dave told Mum and Dad about what happened in Ireland. About his friend shooting the little boy.

Mum said, "Thank God we live here."

Dad said, "There's no guarantee it won't be happening here next."

Mum said to Dave, "Where will you go now?" She wanted to change the subject.

"I don't know," Dave said. "London's a sort of anonymous place. I should be able to get by there for a bit. Then maybe I could get to Germany. I've got a girl friend there."

"If she's a good 'un," Dad said, "like my partner here," and he put his arm around Mum and gave her a squeeze, "she'll get you sorted out right. But if she's a bad 'un, you'll be worse off than ever. I've had some bad experience in that line too."

"Haven't we all," said Mum.

"But we've come through the bad times, haven't we, Love. And I hope you do too. Maybe you and your girl could get to Sweden. I think they'd look after you there."

"Yeah, maybe," Dave said. "Except she's married."

Dad shook his head. "You've certainly got some problems," he said.

"If you go to Germany, Dave," I said, "you could work on a barge. They still have great big barges, and they go up and down the rivers, all through Holland and Germany and Switzerland. A man told me on a boat."

"I know," said Dave. "I've seen them. But I think I've had enough of rivers to last me for a bit."

160

When it came nearly time for Dave's train, Dad helped him into the station, and we all went with him, carrying his bags. Dad gave him a load of money. I think it was twenty pounds. Dave bought his ticket and we all went down to the platform. We didn't have to buy platform tickets. The man let us through without.

"Don't stop to wave," Dave said. He shook hands with Mum and Dad and said, "Thank you." Then he hugged and kissed each one of us in turn. He said, "Thank you. You've been real blood brothers and sisters to me. You're the best friends anybody could ever have. Thank you." Then he looked as though he was going to break down and cry. His lip trembled, and he bit it. "There's one thing," he said. "One thing I wasn't completely honest with you about. It wasn't my mate who shot the little boy in Ireland. It was me." And he hugged me to him, and kissed the top of my head. "It could of been you, Andy," he said. "It could of been you."

Then he let go of me. "Good-by," he said. "And thank you for being my friends."

"Good-by," I said.

And my dad said, "I hope you find your way out to a better place."

Then we walked away. At the top of the stairs I looked back. Dave stood with his back to us. One leg off the ground. Holding on to a post.

That was three years ago now. We've never seen him again. Or heard from him. I don't play with Terry much anymore. Christine passed her qualifying exam and she goes to a new school for smart kids. Lucy's parents took her off to New Zealand. They didn't ask her if she wanted to go. That's the trouble with some parents. They never ask what the kids want. I took my qualifying exam this year. I failed it. But I wouldn't want to go to a school like the one Christine goes to anyway. It's horrible there. She has hours of homework every night. My dad says it's disgusting that they still have them sort of schools and the qualifiers, but they still do here. After the summer I'll have to go to a new school, too, but not Chris's.

I went for a walk along by the canal today with Spotty Sally. Past the bridge where the little boy from our street fell in and was drowned. Where the mill was is just a huge flat dirt place now. They haven't built anything else there. And they haven't rebuilt where the houses were either. The little row of four where Dave lived is still standing. There's ivy growing on the wall at the back of the yard now, where we used to climb over. And there's a tall weed growing just inside the window of the room where Dave stayed. A seed must have blown in, or a bird took it in I suppose. Or maybe one of us carried the seed in on our clothes when we used to go to see him.

I went into the house. You can just walk in through the back door now, because kids have knocked the bricks down. Inside it's much worse than it was then. All the plaster's down, and the cables are ripped out, and there's plaster and laths and rubble all up the stairs so you can hardly walk.

There's all sorts of rubbish in the rooms. Old beer cans and cigarette packs and burnt paper where kids have tried to set fire to the place. Some of the roof tiles are off, and part of the ceiling's down, and all the floor's wet. It was sort of sad going back there on my own. I looked out through the green leaves of the plant, over the canal. There was some kids playing soldiers over where the mill used to be. They were pretending to shoot each other. Some of them fell down, pretending to be wounded or dead.

After supper that night, Dad was sitting on the settee reading my comic. Mum was at the table, playing cards with Christine. I went and sat beside him. He put his arm around me. "What's the matter with you, glum-bum?" he said.

"I've been thinking about Dave."

"Dave?"

"Yeah. You know."

"Oh, *that* Dave. The deserter."

"Why do you think he's never got in touch?" I said. "Do you think he's all right?"

Dad looked at me as though he couldn't

make up his mind whether to say something or not.

"You can't tell," he said after a bit. "Anything could of happened, couldn't it? He might of got off to Germany and be living with his girl. He might still be in London and be doing all right. Or he might of been caught. If he was caught, he'd still be in prison now. Army prisons are worse than ordinary prisons—and they're bad enough."

"Have you ever been in prison, Dad?"

"No. I was one of the lucky ones. I went to visit my mate, Alan, in prison once though. That was enough for me. He was one of the boys in the Home with me. You know what it's like in them Children's Homes. There's a lot of you—all boys or all girls—all shut up together, with a couple of grown-ups who get paid to keep you in order and punish you if you don't obey all the rules and do what they want. And there's nobody there who loves you, or who's got any time to spare for you. Lots of the kids from the Homes end up in prison, or being alcoholics, or junkies. We left the

Home when we were sixteen. I didn't see Alan after that for about nine years. Then I met him one day in London. We recognized each other. After all that time. He was taking drugs then. He was in a terrible state. He was thin as a stray cat. He was covered in sores and scabs. His hands used to shake all the time. His eyes and nose were running. He'd just been thrown out of the place where he was living. See, he never paid any rent. He used to use all his money for the drugs. So him and his wife came and lived with me. She was taking drugs and all. And just after that, he got arrested for selling drugs and sent to prison. I went to see him once. And then he hung himself in his cell."

Dad looked at me again with that same look, as if he was wondering whether to go on. Christine and Mum had stopped playing cards, and were listening. But Dad went on talking just to me. "His wife was really shaken by that. She stayed with me then, and I tried to look after her. Then she got pregnant. That was your mother. She seemed to be getting better. She kept off the drugs while she was pregnant with you. But after you were born she started on the drugs again, more and more. Then, as you know, she went off and left us. I couldn't keep her off the drugs. I don't know where she ever went."

I knew about my mum's going off. But I hadn't known it was because of drugs. Or about Dad's friend in prison. Dad squeezed me tight to him. "And we were just you and me then, Andy. We just had each other. Till we met Mum and Christine. And then we made a real nice family, didn't we. We have our ups and downs. But I love you. All of you. I mean, if I was in prison, I'd never do that, what Alan did. I've got you. I've got something to live for. With something like that you can go through lots of suffering. But if you've got nothing, nobody, what's the point?"

"Did Dave kill himself, Dad?"

"I don't suppose so. I hope he's come through all right. But I'm just telling you . . . I don't know really. You see if they did catch him, they'd treat him pretty badly. And that would make him uglier than when you knew him. There's a lot of ugliness in the world, Andy. Too many people want to pretend it's not there. A lot of people wouldn't agree with me talking to you about things like this. But it's what's there, in the world. I think that's why Dave told you about killing the little boy in Ireland. He wanted you to know the truth."

"Well, I'm glad he told me," I said. "And I hope he writes soon. He should do. We *are* blood brothers."

Format by Gloria Bressler
Set in 13 pt. Janson
Composed, and bound by The Haddon Craftsmen, Scranton, Penna.
Printed by The Murray Printing Co.
HARPER & ROW, PUBLISHERS, INCORPORATED